COLD PINNACLE

a serial killer thriller

PHINEAS AND LIAM, BOOK FOUR

V. J. Chambers

Punk Rawk Books

COLD PINNACLE

a serial killer thriller

PHINEAS AND LIAM, BOOK FOUR

I: HAYSLE DAWSON

CHAPTER ONE

DAWSON WENT INTO the room as Detective Dawson of the Cape Christopher Police Department, a professional captured by some psychotic killer, and she came out Haysle, a bedraggled being who felt less than human.

It was so fast, how all of it was stripped away from her.

So easily done too.

Maybe it was because of getting her period.

Destiny couldn't have known that would happen, and it couldn't have been part of her plan, so it was just an accident that it did, but it was certainly assistive in the entire process of breaking her down. It was a bodily function, a gross one, and being unable to do anything about it, being forced to bleed all over herself alone in that room, it was degrading.

Haysle didn't know how long she was in the room.

There was no way to figure time in the room because there were no windows. It was a small, dingy concrete room, about five feet by five feet square, and there was a toilet in there but no sink.

It might have been more degrading if there hadn't been a toilet, but that would have meant someone had to clean up the filth in the room, Haysle supposed, so maybe that was why she was in a room with a toilet. She didn't know.

There was a light fixture overhead that shone all the time. She had no means of turning it off. It was encased in a metal cage, as if it needed protection from her. This confused her, and she spent far too long contemplating the light. Was there some way to *use* the light fixture? If she got into it, got that cage off, was that the key to her escape?

But she stopped thinking like that shockingly quickly into the imprisonment, and she kept telling herself that—out loud, because she started talking to herself out loud far too soon as well.

"I can't have been in here that long," she would say again and again. "I can't be this far gone yet."

It was only solitude and a lack of food and a lack of sleep.

There was water—in the toilet—and she caved to drinking that more quickly than she would have thought.

The light was always on, and there was nowhere comfortable in the concrete room, but she could have slept, except that every few hours, there was loud awful music that was piped into the room. She would hear someone come by sometimes, see movement under the door to the room, a shadow of legs or feet, and then the music would start.

One of these times, after she started her period, she'd yelled to the person out there about it, begging for sanitary products.

Of course, the person didn't acknowledge her.

She did sleep—a little—short naps in between being wrenched awake by the loud music. She had water to drink. But she was hungry and she was alone and then she was bleeding and then…

Her period coming was another way she knew she couldn't have been in there that long, because it was due. It was late, in fact. She had distrusted her two negative pregnancy tests because of its not making an appearance, and now it was here, so it could have been a matter of days, and yet, she was already so far gone, and so desperate.

The hunger was very bad at first, and then she went through a phase in which she could hardly feel it but during which she was very alert, and this was the time when she spent a lot of time scheming over the light overhead, babbling to herself, wondering aloud about Liam—

Was Liam in a room like this?

Where was Liam?

Where were they?

They'd been taken here in a car, at gunpoint, after they'd set up a failed sting operation to catch Destiny Worth. Instead, Phineas Slater had escaped, and two of Destiny's lackeys had shot at them, subdued them, and taken them captive.

Then they drove for a long time, but with canvas bags over their heads so that they couldn't see where they were being taken, and then they were separated, and she was taken to this room, and now, she had lost her mind.

After a while, the alert phase waned, and she grew weak. The weakness was exacerbated by the lack of sleep, and she felt as if she deteriorated very rapidly. Frighteningly rapidly.

The worst thing wasn't the hunger or lack of sleep though, it was the solitude.

No one there. Nothing to do. Only her thoughts to keep her company.

At first, she thought that talking to herself would keep her sane and help her feel as if she weren't alone, but soon she began to realize she was dissociating and becoming confused and that the environment had taken her apart.

And then, her period.

She was glad.

She didn't want to be pregnant in this place. She didn't want to know what starvation and sleep deprivation would do to a growing fetus. She was glad.

She didn't allow herself to think that maybe it wasn't her period but a very early miscarriage, likely brought on by the starvation and sleep deprivation, because what did that matter? The result was the same.

Well.

She didn't *mean* to allow herself to think things, but she had nothing *but* her thoughts.

There was a phase—early on—where she'd tried to assure herself that someone was coming for them. She'd had a theory, that Quentin Worth, Destiny's brother, must have come from Destiny's location, and that all they had to do was trace his phone's movement and the police would come straight here and rescue them.

But she began to realize that she had no idea if this was true.

Destiny—well, the Worth family—had properties all over the country, and there was no saying where they'd been taken. Destiny also used properties owned by members of her cult, people who she had gathered from the MadCad fandom.

MadCad was what fans called the slash pairing of Maddox and Cade from the YA book *Dusk*. The pairing had a devoted following with lots of art, fanfiction, and other works, even though the two were not romantically involved in the original work.

Destiny had an expensive course online, claiming that it would teach people how to make MadCad art, sell it at conventions, and amass a lot of money. But it was only the first of her attempts to gain control of people, and once she had them in the class, she would convince some of them to come and be with her, and these followers became so devoted that they were willing to kill themselves—even eager and determined to do so.

Haysle couldn't understand it.

And then one day, she opened her eyes after a short nap in the room and a box of tampons was sitting on the concrete in front of her, and she started to sob in gratefulness and relief.

This is how Stockholm syndrome works, said a dull voice in her brain.

She knew that.

She didn't care.

She was incredibly grateful to whoever had given her these tampons. They were her dignity, her personhood, and she had that back.

THEN THE TAMPONS disappeared.

It happened the same way, while she was sleeping.

It shouldn't have mattered, really, because she was at the tail end of her cycle, and her flow had gotten to the point where it was that light brownish blood, hardly enough to stain her pants or underwear — though she had washed them out in the toilet more than once and then shivered in them cold and wet. She didn't like the idea of being naked in this room, though — it was too much to bear — too vulnerable.

But it *did* matter.

It was her dignity gone.

It was the one kind and good thing that had happened to her taken from her for no reason.

She felt like it broke her.

She didn't cry, but she was devastated all the same.

She went… not catatonic, though maybe it would have appeared that way, but she stopped talking aloud to herself and stopped trying to clean her clothes and simply sprawled in a corner of the room.

She had given up.

Eventually, she fell asleep again, and when she woke up, the door was open.

IT WAS DARK outside of the room, pitch black dark and the only light was illuminated from the open door of her little room, a place she had somehow oddly begun to think of as safe, as a home of sorts.

She didn't want to leave that room.

How fucked up was that?

She'd been starved and imprisoned and now the door was open and she —

"Yes, but it's a trick," she whispered.

It had to be a trick. There was no reason that they would leave the door open, but they did. And she stayed inside for a long, long time.

She ventured out the door, into the hallway, to the edge of the light and then retreated. During these excursions, she realized her pants no longer stayed up on her body. She had lost a lot of weight.

Haysle was a naturally thin sort of person, though that was changing a bit in her thirties, and she was getting a bit soft around the middle. Going off of testosterone had changed her body as well, making it fleshier and rounder.

There was nothing round about her anymore.

She surveyed her arms and her belly, and she was skeletal. This frightened her and she retreated back into her room.

She huddled in the corner and cried again. It was ridiculous. Why couldn't she walk out into that darkness? Why couldn't she run?

It was most certainly a trick, but she was beginning to think she understood the trick, and the trick was just to show her how broken she was, and how much she had been dismantled.

See? I don't have to lock you up anymore. I can keep you prisoner just fine now. I own you now.

This thought was the thought that finally galvanized her.

She got up and darted out of the room, darting out into the darkness.

Then she had to pause and haul up her pants. She folded them over and rolled them at the waist, like pegging one's jeans' legs, something her older aunt had showed her once when she was a very little girl. *We used to do this when I was a teenager, and sometimes the end of the pant leg would be so tight you could hardly fold it.*

The thought of a time before, back when she had been a person with family, who wasn't falling apart, frightened of the dark, huddling in her prison like some pathetic animal, it tore into her and forced her on.

She went down dark corridors, and she couldn't see anything. There were doors sometimes, but they were always locked.

Then, up ahead, she saw light, and she ran for it.

A stairwell.

She was in a basement, and the stairs were open, just flat,

unfinished boards with no risers. The steps were illuminated overhead by a faint light. She climbed up those steps to the door at the top and tried the knob, expecting it to be locked.

But it wasn't, and it turned in her hands, and she emerged into a kitchen.

It was massive and modern, with an expanse of granite-covered island counter space in the middle and high white cabinets with silver knobs, gleaming appliances, a toaster tucked near the sink, an air fryer next to it, and a silver blender that caught the sunlight from the windows.

The sun was so bright that she cringed from it, feeling like some subterranean creature that had come up from the sewers to come upon civilization. It all felt vaguely theatrical, even, as if she'd seen this in a movie before, maybe many movies but in different contexts, and they swam in her brain, as she wondered if she were a victim or a monster or a vampire herself—like Cade from *Dusk*.

She looked around for a door to the outside.

There wasn't one.

She could maybe open one of the windows and hurl herself out it. Or maybe she throw the toaster at it and—

She thought of the noise, the shards of glass, trying to haul her weak body up onto the countertops.

She staggered across the kitchen instead and leaned against the island, and then she spied a loaf of bread sitting out next to the toaster and she snatched it up with trembling fingers.

She fumbled with the twist-tie that held it closed.

And then it slipped out of her hands and fell on the floor, the tie coming loose, the bread spilling out on the linoleum, three pieces on the floor. She snatched them up, not even bothering to worry about dirt, and stuffed them into her mouth.

Clutching the loaf of bread, chewing, she made her way out of the kitchen.

The kitchen opened onto a hallway. It was dark—wood paneling on the walls, but not the flimsy kind of the 1970s and 80s, the dignified board-and-batten style of the 1800s.

Between that and the look of the wood floor at her feet, she began to think this was a very old house.

She kept eating bread and moving down the hallway.

Doorways opened onto various rooms—many of them empty, some with discarded pieces of furniture, one with a collection of exercise equipment, but—

No door.

No way out.

And then, eventually, she came to the end of the hallway, and there was a staircase to her left, the side covered in that same dark wood paneling, ascending into the top of the house and right at the foot of the steps was the *front door.*

She lurched forward and found the knob.

It turned, and she opened the door, and the cool autumn wind blew inside, and outside there was a tree with a few brown leaves clinging to its branches and a front porch with a swing on it, and Liam was there.

She started at the sight of him.

His hair was longer, curling around his ears, and he had a straggly kind of beard on his gaunt face and his eyes were hollow. He met her gaze for a second, but he was blank, and he looked away.

"Haysle," said a female voice. "There you are."

Haysle turned and Destiny Worth was sitting on the porch swing. She had a pistol in her lap. It was pointed at Haysle, but Destiny wasn't holding it. It was just sitting there, balanced on Destiny's thighs as she lightly swung back and forth on the swing.

Haysle didn't know what to do. She wanted to go to Liam and take his face in her hands and ask him what they had done to him and if he was okay.

But she only hugged the loaf of bread to her chest and gaped at Destiny.

"Come here," said Destiny, beckoning to her, smiling reassuringly.

Somehow, it didn't occur to her to refuse, and she took several unsteady steps toward the porch swing.

Immediately, Liam scurried into the door behind her, his

head down.

Haysle let out a noise, turning in his wake.

"Come here," said Destiny again.

Haysle licked her lips and looked back at Destiny.

Destiny's smile was gentle. "You must be hungry."

Haysle shook. Yes, she was hungry, and that was because Destiny had locked her in a room with no food for a long enough time that the trees had lost all their leaves, so... what? A month?

No, it must be sooner, because her period, it had been going to come any day, and if it was *that* late, that would mean—

Liam.

She wanted to turn to look after him again, but she didn't. She swallowed. "Are you going to make me go back in there?"

"That's really up to you, Haysle," said Destiny. "As long as I can trust you, you can go anywhere you want. Can I trust you enough?"

"Trust me to... to what?"

"To stay put," said Destiny, smiling wider. "It's really for your own good to be here. I know you didn't start our program by choice, so we've have to take some extraordinary steps with you. We had to brute force our way in and destroy your poisonous ego, break you down, take you down to the studs." She laughed, but it was warm. "Now, we can start rebuilding. You're on your way to becoming your best self, you know?"

This was... this was weird cult-like... Haysle swallowed. "I don't want to go back in that room. And I want my tampons back."

"Of course," said Destiny. "So, you won't try anything, then?"

Haysle shook her head.

Destiny reached down and stroked the pistol. "I could tell you that this property is surrounded by a fence with alarms and that all of my faithful are armed and willing to protect me with their lives. I could tell you that trying to go anywhere would be futile. But I don't even think I need to tell you those things, do I, Haysle? You just want some food and a shower and some clothes that fit."

Haysle felt tears coming to her eyes. She did want those things, so badly that it made her feel as if she might break into little pieces.

"And your tampons back," said Destiny, smiling. She stood up from the swing. "Come on then, I'll take you to your room." She tucked the pistol into a holster on her belt and went inside, leaving Haysle alone on the porch.

Haysle looked out at the yard there, covered in fallen leaves, and the trees, and the little stone walkway that curved through the yard, and the driveway, black-topped, winding between the trees.

She didn't see a fence.

She saw herself jumping off the porch and making a run for it.

But she was weak and tired and underfed, and Destiny had a gun, and she imagined that would end with her getting shot in the back and dying, and —

She turned around and followed Destiny back into the house.

"Shut the door," called Destiny, who was already halfway up the steps.

Haysle shut it.

CHAPTER TWO

HAYSLE STAYED IN the shower for a long time, sitting on the floor next to the drain, hugging her knees to her chest, the water pounding down on her back.

The water was warm and good and she didn't know if she'd felt anything quite so pleasurable in her life.

When she got out, she was given clothing and food, and Monique was there. Monique was one of the people who had captured them and forced them into the car at gunpoint. Haysle only knew her name because Slater had said it.

Where was Slater?

Where was Liam?

She thought about asking questions and then thought about being shut back in that room downstairs and she didn't say anything.

Monique talked, however, hovering next to her as she ate. They were in a room that had two sets of bunk beds and Monique had told her the upper bunk closest to the window would be Haysle's and that Monique would sleep beneath her. Haysle didn't know why she had to eat in the bedroom, but maybe they didn't trust her to be in other rooms in the house yet. Would she eat all her meals there? She didn't care. She was glad to have food.

"I always felt alone, you know?" Monique said, watching her. "No matter who was around, no matter what was going on. I was in a bad way. I had a problem with prescription drugs, and I'd been to rehab twice, and I couldn't kick the habit. And then I met Destiny."

Right, this was typical cult stuff, right? Destiny had "fixed" Monique.

"I didn't even go through withdrawal," said Monique. "She did some hypnosis on me, and my addiction just went away."

Hypnosis? Well, that was a thought, wasn't it?

Of course, maybe that was all cults were, mass hypnosis. Haysle knew that a common way to break a person down was to use hunger and sleep deprivation, and…

It works. It really works.

She wanted to cry.

She was too hungry to cry. She simply ate.

"She saved my life," said Monique. "I know you're hostile to the cause, but I want you to understand that Destiny is a force for good. You might not be able to see it yet, but I know you will soon."

Haysle thought of arguments, questions she could ask. If Destiny was such a force for good, why did she kill people? If Destiny was so great, why did she need a group of people following her around, propping up her ego? But she remembered a conversation she'd had with a cult deprogrammer named Mercedes Gibson, and she knew that she needed to establish a rapport first before she could do anything to challenge Monique's convictions.

Besides, she needed to appear compliant.

It's a strategy, she told herself, shoveling rice into her mouth. *I can't get free from that room in the basement, but up here, I have range of movement, and I can make a plan. I have to play along and make friends.*

Yes, it was a strategy, and she wasn't already broken somewhere deep in her mind and too frightened to even try to escape. She had to believe that, she supposed.

Haysle set down her spoon and eyed Monique. She noted she hadn't been given a fork. Guess they didn't trust her that much. She tried to smile at the woman. "You, um, that shirt is pretty."

Monique looked down at her shirt, which was just a teal t-shirt. She gave Haysle a shy smile. "I like this color."

"Me too," said Haysle. She swallowed. "Uh, you know, you seem like a good person deep down. Maybe, um, maybe I was wrong about everything. I… I'm willing to give it all a chance."

"That's great," said Monique. "Maybe it will all work out then. We've lost a lot of members of the family lately, and Destiny says we need new blood, but I didn't think she'd be able to convince a police detective to… but I shouldn't have doubted her."

"You, uh, you really admire her?"

"I love her," said Monique. "I'm devoted to her. I'd do anything for her."

Even kill yourself, thought Haysle.

Monique reached out and put a hand on Haysle's hand. "But we'd all do anything for each other here, because we're a family, and that's what you do for family. Furthermore, we're all here in the service of love, and it's only noble to sacrifice for love."

The highest form of love is sacrifice. It was a catch-phrase of Destiny's weird cult.

"It can be like that for you too. You're here with us now, and we'll welcome you into our family. We're all about acceptance here."

Haysle ate more rice.

Monique got up from where she sat and went across the room. She opened up a closet and pulled out another shirt, a different style and a slightly different shade but still teal. "Do you want this one? You can wear it if you want. What belongs to one person in the family belongs to all of us."

In spite of herself, Haysle felt touched by this gesture. Monique barely knew her and she was being so nice.

She tried to remind herself that Monique had nearly shot them both to death but all of that seemed as if it was long ago, beyond a barrier, another time, another person, back when she was Dawson, when she had respect, when she didn't feel nearly moved to tears by the offering of teal tshirts.

"Thank you," whispered Haysle, taking the shirt.

THERE WERE TWO other girls that stayed in the room with Haysle and Monique. Their names were Kyleigh and Pam, and Haysle called them girls, but it was only because they all seemed somewhat infantalized somehow, all of them gaunt and wide-eyed in clothes that fell off their skeletal frames, all of them whispering and tentative and somehow broken, too, broken down like she was. However, she wouldn't have been surprised to learn they were also in their thirties or even forties. She simply couldn't tell, however, and she didn't ask.

Haysle was very grateful to have a bed to slip into that night, a place to relax, somewhere soft, with blankets and a pillow, but she was stunned when she was awakened while it was still dark outside to the sound of the same type of music that had been pumped into her room downstairs.

At first, she was disoriented, unsure where she was, and it was only the flutter of movement around her that made her realize she was upstairs in this room with these other girls, who were all up and out of bed and beginning to do something that resembled the Sun Salutation, a vaguely yoga-like set of movements that they performed together in front of the bunks.

Monique seized her and pulled her over, whispering to follow her lead, and she would get it.

It was true. By the fifth or sixth iteration of the movement, Haysle was well-versed in how to stretch and move, bending down and reaching up, even breathing with the other women.

They did it for at least a half hour.

Then, abruptly, the music stopped and they all returned to bed.

Haysle followed suit, but when she lay down in bed, she noticed that door to the bedroom was open, and she began to visualize herself slowly and carefully climbing out of the bed and tiptoeing across the room and going through the door. She visualized herself sneaking out of the house and getting free, flagging down a car, calling for help, bringing back someone to save them all.

Her visualizations turned to dreams, and she dreamed that she got free only to find herself back in the room downstairs, drinking water out of the toilet.

When she was jolted awake to the sound of an alarm, it was only then that she realized she'd fallen asleep.

The other girls were getting up and making their beds.

Haysle got up too. It wasn't easy to make the top bunk, but she managed it.

The girls ducked into the attached bathroom and ran wet combs through their hair and brushed their teeth.

"We take showers in the evening," Monique said. "You're the newest, so you'll be last, after Kyleigh." She guided Haysle out of the room and back downstairs, to the kitchen. She gave Haysle a canister of something that looked like flour and told her it was homemade pancake mix, and to mix three cups with water and make pancakes.

Haysle stood at the stove for some time, making pancake after pancake, stacking the cooked ones on plates that were whisked away.

Eventually, when all the pancake mix was gone, Haysle was allowed to sit down in the dining room with Monique and Kyleigh, and there was one pancake left for each of them. There had been other things for breakfast—bacon and eggs and some bananas—but all of those things had been eaten by other people who Haysle hadn't seen. She had no idea how many people were in this house.

Haysle ate the pancake without butter and with the scant amount of syrup that Monique said they were each allowed, and she was hungry.

She was free of the room, she supposed, but now she was just in a bigger prison, and she wasn't being starved anymore, but she wasn't going to be fed well either.

It's all right. I'm biding my time. I'm looking for my chance to escape, she told herself.

"We're on dishes today," said Monique, scooting out her chair and taking Haysle's plate as she got up.

"We cooked," said Haysle.

"It's a schedule," said Monique. "Sometimes we end up with double kitchen duty. You'll figure it out eventually."

"Is it posted somewhere?" said Haysle.

"Nope," said Monique, smiling and tapping her temple. "But we've all got it right here. You will too."

No, I won't be here long enough.

When they got into the kitchen, Haysle stopped short.

Phineas Slater was bent over the counter wearing a tight gray t-shirt that clung to his chest and arms. Did he seem thinner too, or was she imagining things? He was watching the toaster, and he glanced up at her, and then a smile spread over his face. "Haysle, look at you."

Haysle backed away, too many awful memories surfacing in her head — the video she'd once watched of one of Slater's murders, him sliding a knife into a woman's skull, Slater in her apartment ordering her to eat for him, Slater looking at Liam and Liam looking back at him and —

She might have whimpered.

He prowled across the room to her.

"I thought that Destiny said that you were supposed to be in the attic," said Monique coldly.

Slater ignored Monique and advanced on Haysle, who collided painfully with the corner of a countertop and winced, rubbing her hip bone. When she looked up, Slater was close, too close.

He leaned down and whispered in her ear, "He'd want me to tell you we're working on it."

Her eyes widened.

"I don't think Destiny wants you near her," said Monique.

Across the room, the toaster popped up, and Slater whirled. "You still hungry, Haysle?"

"Destiny —"

"Is not in here," said Slater, rounding on Monique, who

cowered from him. Slater stalked across the room. "I make a mean avocado toast if you're interested."

"You want to watch me eat?" Haysle breathed.

He gave her a dark look. "Definitely."

Haysle shuddered. She wrapped her arms around her too-small waist. "Okay," she agreed in a tiny voice. She *was* hungry.

"Excellent," said Slater, pulling the toast out of the toaster. There were four pieces. "You want one too, Monique?"

Monique's nostrils flared. "Destiny—"

Slater gave her a wink. "Come on, live a little."

"I'm not authorized for avocado," whispered Monique. "Neither is Haysle. I'm on a low-fat rotation, and—"

"Fuck that," said Slater. "*Fuck* low fat."

Monique bit down on her bottom lip. "Destiny won't like it."

"You let me deal with her," said Slater. He turned his gaze onto Haysle. "What do you think, Haysle? Allies?" He grinned mischievously.

Haysle swallowed.

Slater sorted through a bowl of fruit on top of the refrigerator and came down with two avocados. The two girls were drawn forward as if by some sorcery and they watched him with open mouths, eager shallow breaths, as he peeled and sliced the avocados and arranged them on the four pieces of toast. He sprinkled them with salt and paprika. He left two on a plate and picked up the other two slices and came around the room, grinning at the girls.

He slid in between them. "One at a time. I'll feed you."

No, thought Haysle.

"Finn." Monique's voice was breathy.

He grinned at Monique. "Haysle first." Then he turned to Haysle. "Open your mouth.

No. She opened her mouth.

He brought the toast close. His voice went low and gravelly. "Take a bite."

She did. It was good. She hadn't had anything as rich as

an avocado in quite some time, and she shut her eyes, letting out a moan in spite of herself as she chewed.

"Haysle." He was suddenly pressed into her, the whole length of his body, which was hard and rippling and strong.

Her eyes snapped open. Her heart started to pound.

He moved the toast close to her mouth again.

She tried to take another bite.

He yanked it away. "Monique's turn," he whispered, turning to the other woman.

Monique opened her mouth obligingly, and he fed her. Then he kissed her.

Haysle shuddered again.

While Slater and Monique's mouths were making sloppy noises against each other, Slater fed Haysle more toast.

She chewed, heart going way too fast in her chest. She was terrified he was going to try to kiss her too. She was terrified because she wouldn't stop him if he did, and she didn't know how she was going to handle that after it was all over, and where that would even leave her.

She was already so broken down, but that would… would…

Slater broke the kiss with Monique and handed Monique her piece of toast. "What do you say?"

"Thank you, Finn," said Monique softly.

Slater used his now-free arm to wrap around Haysle, tugging her tightly against him. It was all intimate now. She was in his arms. Her heart beat like a live thing trying to escape the cage of her ribs.

"Haysle, you want more toast?"

"Yes," she whispered.

"I'll give it to you," he said, "if you say please?"

"Please," she said obediently.

"Say my name," he said hoarsely.

"Please, Slater."

He shook his head. "Come on, Haysle." Now, he was annoyed.

"F-finn," she said. "Please, Finn."

"Good girl." He fed her another bite of toast. "Always call

me Finn from now on, okay?"

She nodded at him, chewing. She had never known avocado toast could taste so good.

Finn rubbed his thumb over her lower lip. "Good girl," he said again, and he handed her the toast to feed herself and let go of her.

She held onto the toast and eyed him.

He gave her a smile—he was handsome, she'd always thought he was handsome—and then he shoved his hands in his pockets and went over to the other pieces of toast, which he began eating himself.

Monique brushed crumbs away from her lips. "We need to start on the dishes."

"Right," said Haysle. She wanted to savor the rest of the toast, but she felt pressure not to. Instead, she shoved the rest of it into her mouth and chewed.

She joined Monique.

When she looked back, Finn was gone, leaving his plate behind with toast crumbs on it.

"Would it have killed him to bring it over to the sink?" said Monique, annoyed. She went over and retrieved it. "Look, you know him, so you know how he is."

"Sort of," said Haysle.

"Destiny lets him get away with murder," said Monique.

And Haysle laughed, because that was literally true.

Well, Finn claimed that Destiny had murdered women for him and gave him the corpses to fuck, and then when he'd gotten good and hooked on necrophilia, she'd refused to give him any more dead girls and forced him to kill them himself, which was how he'd become a serial killer.

Monique blinked at her. "Why are you laughing?"

"Just because he lures prostitutes with fast food and then stabs them in the back of the neck before he fucks every single one of their holes." Oh, why had she said it like that? She'd watched that video, though, all of that in color, right on screen, too real—so real it had seemed fake, the way violence always seemed, like bad special effects, as if real blood couldn't *be* real somehow.

Monique drew back. "What?"

"Don't you know this?" said Haysle, turning back to the sink. She was in the middle of washing while Monique was drying and putting the dishes away. "Why did you think you had to break him out of jail? Why did you think he was locked up?"

"It was a mistake," said Monique. "Whatever he was arrested for."

Haysle shook her head. "He filmed it. I've seen the videos. I *watched him* do it."

Monique looked troubled. She touched her lips, where she'd kissed Finn.

Haysle set another dish in the rack. "Anyway, what were you going to say about him? That you didn't want me to say anything to Destiny about how we ate fat? Because I'm fine with that, if so."

Monique lowered her fingers and eyed the dishes, but she didn't start drying again.

"Would Destiny blame us and not him?"

Monique picked up the towel and briskly began to dry a plate. "No, of course not. Destiny isn't like that. She doesn't blame people. She might sometimes have insight into our own weaknesses and be able to point those out to us to help us grow, but that's not the same thing."

"And with Finn?" said Haysle. "How does she help him grow?"

Monique set down the dried plate with a clatter on a stack of other dried plates. "It's probably better if we don't talk."

Haysle wanted to push, at least part of her did. She didn't push. She just went quiet, did as she was told. She wasn't sure how this could have happened to her, how she could have been so very altered in so short a time.

I'm a detective, she thought to herself. *I get to the bottom of things. I should push.*

She didn't push.

CHAPTER THREE

DAYS PASSED AND despite Monique's assurance that Haysle would begin to understand and anticipate the routine, she did not. The chores seemed to be erratically assigned. They did the dishes two days later, but they cooked breakfast every day, and then they were back on dishes duty for four days after that.

On other days, they had different chores.

They did laundry one day, and they vacuumed the house top to bottom another.

Finally, to Haysle's delight, they were sent outside to gather stray branches from the lawn, things that had fallen from the trees in a recent storm. Anytime she wandered too far, Monique called her back, but Haysle noted that she didn't *see* a fence.

She stood out in the chilly air, arms full of a bundle of sticks, and looked down the winding driveway until it disappeared, and her heart picked up speed as she imagined dropping the sticks and making a run for it now.

Then she turned with her bundle of sticks and went to deposit them in the wheelbarrow.

She didn't see Finn again or Liam again, not for some time.

She did see Destiny a few times, but Destiny didn't speak to her. She moved amongst Monique and Kyleigh and Pam wordlessly now and again.

The meditation drills didn't happen every night. (Haysle had learned that's what it was called when they had to get up and do yoga to raucous music in the middle of the night.) They were random as near as she could tell. She had yet to experience them two nights in a row, however, not that she thought that meant anything.

Even still, that night, she lay in bed, thinking that there had been a meditation drill the night before and that there wouldn't be one tonight. She lay in bed listening to the even breath of the other women in the room, telling herself that they were all asleep.

She lay in bed and argued with herself.

What about Liam? she asked herself. *I can't leave Liam.*

But she was no good to Liam here, not like this, and if she got free, she could bring back help.

So, eventually, she very carefully climbed down out of her bunk and put her bare feet on the hardwood floor and eyed the other girls in the room, eyed their motionless, sleeping forms.

She tiptoed over to find the pair of dilapidated boots she'd been given and she picked them up. She carried them out of the room, walking on her tiptoes, carefully darting over the floor.

It creaked when she went through the doorway and into the hallway.

Her breath caught and she froze.

She peered back into the room, but none of the girls had stirred. She looked out into the hallway, but it was dark and still.

She kept going.

She scampered silently down the hallway and to the stairwell and then she went down the steps.

They creaked badly — loudly — and she cringed with each careful step she took, trying to step towards the edges, to some spot that would not creak, but every spot creaked.

She was sure that someone was going to rush out — either at the top of the steps or the bottom — and she imagined being shoved down into the basement and back into that room where she'd been kept.

The toilet in there seemed to smile in her mind's eye, a dingy porcelain monster ready to swallow her.

She gritted her teeth and rushed down the rest of the steps as quickly as she could, not trying to mitigate the noise, and then she hurried over to the front door.

It was locked, the deadbolt turned over, but she unlocked the deadbolt and opened the door.

The bottom of the door came free with a loud sound, and she jumped.

She didn't wait to see if anyone was coming, however. She simply hurled herself out that door and onto the porch and took off running.

She was halfway down the driveway before she stopped to put on her boots.

She was freezing. It was incredibly cold out here and she hadn't stopped for a jacket, though they'd all been hanging on a rack next to the front door, right there, easily taken, easily shrugged into, and then she wouldn't be so cold, but she hadn't done it, and it was too late now.

She tied the boots tight and took off running again.

She ran and ran until the house was far behind her, swallowed into the darkness.

This driveway, it must be over a mile long, because it kept going and going, and she was soon too exhausted to run any longer. She had never been much for exercise, finding it painful. Being a naturally thin person anyway, nothing had ever forced her into doing it for health reasons. She wasn't in very good shape, and her body had also been through hell just recently, what with the starvation and the lack of sleep.

She slowed to a walk, panting loudly, her breaths so loud that they seemed to echo off the surrounding trees and the night sky above.

She was less frightened that anyone could hear her now that she was this far away from the house, but she began to wonder about other things, suddenly.

Finn had been obsessed with cameras. He'd documented everything, and the case against him had been so airtight primarily because of all of the video evidence. He could never have wiggled out of it.

Why had he done that?

If he wasn't the mastermind, and Destiny was, as Finn claimed, then had the cameras been her idea? And if so, were there cameras out here?

She looked up at the trees surrounding the driveway, looking for little blinking red lights, even though she knew that obvious cameras were often put there just to frighten people into behaving and often didn't even work. Real surveillance cameras were not easily discovered by a casual visual search.

And that was when the fence came into view, and she stopped short.

It was made of wrought iron and it was eight feet tall. The black posts were two inches apart, each topped with a decorative arrow shape at the top. The fence had a scalloped edge at the top, each fence section making a U shape with two high spikes on each end. It was a nice-looking fence, like something one might see surrounding a posh gated community, not around a cult compound. Owing to the fact that there were only two horizontal metal braces, one at the bottom and one at the top, it wasn't climbable.

She could see that the gate was locked.

And then she heard a rustling, and she whirled, looking for movement.

There.

A man emerged from the darkness, someone Haysle had seen before but whose name she didn't know. She hadn't been introduced to everyone, after all. There weren't a lot of people living here, all told. Maybe ten, not counting Destiny and Finn.

The man had a gun strapped to him, a shoulder holster over his clothes. He hadn't drawn it, but it was very prominent.

He came for her.

She wanted to run, but she didn't. He had a gun, and he could shoot her in the back, and she was…

Well, she'd gambled and lost.

There was a fence, and it was guarded, and she was going back into the hole in the basement, a sacrifice to the toilet there, and she knew this had been her one chance, because after another session of solitude with no food, she would be utterly destroyed. She would never attempt escape again.

Tears began to fall silently down her cheeks. She didn't bother to wipe them away.

The man with the gun didn't say anything. He came to her and took her by the arm and started to drag her back toward the house, and she didn't fight him, because she didn't want to get shot, and because she was already broken. She was a mouse now, not a police detective.

Not Dawson. Haysle.

The tears kept coming, but she didn't sob. Her breath didn't hitch.

Halfway to the house, the tears stopped. She had started to shiver because of the cold, and her teeth were chattering. Maybe she couldn't shiver and cry at the same time.

When they approached the house, someone was on the porch smoking a cigarette, and all she could see was the glowing tip of it.

Then whoever it was jumped down and hurried over to them. As the figure approached, she recognized it as Finn.

"Hey," said Finn to the man with the gun. "Mick, you want a smoke?"

The man with the gun, Mick apparently, let go of Haysle's arm. "I'm on a no-tobacco rotation."

"I won't tell." Finn tugged a pack of cigarettes out of the pocket in his hoodie. It was crushed and misshapen. He opened it and held it out to the other man. "Go for it."

Mick hesitated and then took the cigarette.

Finn handed him a lighter, absently rolling his own cigarette butt until the cherry fell off onto the driveway. He tucked the butt back into the pack and put the pack away. "So, uh, how about you do me a solid and just don't say anything about this." He reached out and snatched Haysle away from Mick, pulling her against his body.

"What? You think a cigarette buys my silence? She tried to leave. That's an act of aggression. It requires intense sessions to correct. Destiny needs to know."

"I'll give her an intense session," said Finn.

"You don't—"

"I'm saying she won't try it again," said Finn, slinging an arm around Haysle's shoulders.

"If Destiny finds out—"

"I'll deal with Destiny," said Finn.

Mick sucked on his cigarette and surveyed Finn. Then he slowly let out the smoke. "You leave me out of it entirely. I never saw her. I was never here. I never—"

"Yes," said Finn.

"Whatever," said Mick and turned around and walked off into the night.

Haysle swallowed, watching him go. Being this close to Finn was making her body do spasmy things. She wasn't shivering anymore, because she was close to him, and his body heat was warming her, but her heart had started to pound savagely, and she looked up at him, her body jerking in ways that weren't shivers, but were… were…

Finn cupped her face with one massive hand. "You need to shave, don't you?" He rubbed his thumb over the sideburn area of Haysle's face. "It's very light, almost like peachfuzz. You can't really see it, but I can *feel* it. Funny. I see why Liam likes it, actually. On you, it's…" He let out a soft laugh.

This was not making her feel more safe. She jerked again. "No," she said, but it was voiceless.

"What's that?"

"Please," she said, and even to her own ears, the pitch of her voice was just too deep to be properly vulnerable. She couldn't beg him. It wouldn't work. She jerked again.

He tightened his grip on her. "You're shivering. Let's get you inside."

She stumbled when he walked, but then she knew she had to do as he wished and walk with him, because he was stronger than her, and she thought wistfully of taking testosterone and how much easier it was to put on muscle and that phase she'd gone through of lifting weights to make her feel more masculine, even though it never worked—not because she didn't seem masculine but because some part of her had always recoiled from her masculinity, had felt as if it were wrong because she had never been trans.

Even so, it would be better if she were stronger.

He yanked her through the house, all the way through the kitchen and to a set of stairs that were small and narrow and steep—probably a set of servants' stairs. It *was* an old house.

They climbed and climbed, all the way to the tiptop of the house, to a room where the roof sloped on either side and where there was a mattress on the floor. The covers were askew and the sheets were stained. Food stains, most likely, she thought idly.

He pushed her at the bed.

She staggered and her knees collided with it, and she knew this was when she needed to fight him.

"Lie down, Haysle," he said.

"No," she said hoarsely. She glanced over her shoulder at the stairs and then at him.

He shoved her.

She fell into the mattress face first and she just lay there and jerked and didn't fight him, didn't even *try*.

He settled down at the end of the mattress and lit another cigarette. "You can't *do* that, Haysle," he said.

Her voice came out steady, as if it were detached from her, some separate element from herself. "Do what?"

"Try to leave," he said. "You'll make Destiny mad, and she'll put you back downstairs, and that will make Liam mad, and he's getting cooperative."

"Oh, is he?" Somehow, she managed to sound aloof and amused. "Well, I wouldn't want to stand in the way of that."

"You wouldn't, actually," said Finn. "Because that's how we all get what we want."

"Am I included in this 'we'?"

"You want to go home, right?" said Finn. "Liam and I are working on it. But you have to not fuck things up."

"Working on it how?"

"Liam is making Destiny happy, if you catch my drift," said Finn. "Why do you think she let you out of the hole?"

Haysle's stomach roiled. What? Liam was trading sexual favors for her freedom? No. She didn't want—

"So, Destiny makes all this noise about abstaining from sex to sharpen you and make you into your best self?" Finn ashed his cigarette into his palm and then squinted at it, annoyed. He rubbed his hand on the sheets of the mattress and got up. "Most of the women here, they've been celibate for years, but Destiny always wants to fuck *all* the men. It's like a big secret, but I know everything." He bent down and snatched up an ashtray from the floor. "They're not allowed to fuck anyone else besides her, and they aren't allowed to talk about it, but they have to fuck her."

Haysle tried to stand up.

Finn shot over to the bed and put his palm on her back and pushed her back down, gentle but firm.

She let out a noise that sounded vaguely like a sob, but now her eyes were dry.

"On your back," he said, surveying her.

She rolled over, following his orders.

He nodded his approval. "Anyway, she treats me different, but not that different." He blew out smoke. "I'm also only allowed to fuck her, and she's busy a lot of the time." He smashed the cigarette in the ashtray, but it didn't go out entirely and the smoke rose in a wisp.

She watched the smoke while he tugged her pants and underwear down to her knees. She was wearing pajamas. She hadn't bothered with real clothes before the escape attempt.

She thought again about fighting him. She thought she could probably make him not do it. She could rake nails over his face or knee him in the balls or something. She had some hand-to-hand combat training as a police officer, and she knew a thing or two about using an opponent's strength against him.

But it wasn't like the movies, where a person could just

kick a guy and he'd go down, unconscious, and then the heroine could run away. Knocking a guy that hard on the head caused brain damage, and it wasn't easy to accomplish.

So, the best she'd be able to do was incapacitating him enough for her to get away. She would run down the steps and out of the house and…

And go where?

Back to the fence?

Back to Mick and his gun?

She licked her lips and her voice came out dry and amused, that strange voice that didn't belong to her, the wrong voice for this situation, entirely wrong. "You don't have to do this. I won't try to escape again. I can see it's pointless."

Finn pulled her pants and underwear off entirely. "Maybe not. But like I said, I'm a little frustrated, Haysle." He climbed between her thighs. "So, it's for me too. Lie still, please? Will you do that for me?"

"So you can pretend I'm dead?" Her voice was still unemotional.

"Right, you understand," he breathed, his voice threaded with pleasure. He was touching her between her legs now with one hand, and he was unzipping his pants with the other. "Dry as fuck," he muttered. "I'm going to try not to be offended by that."

"All the better to imagine me dead," she told the ceiling.

"True." He leaned over her and sorted through a basket near the top of the mattress. Coming out with a bottle of lube, he settled back onto his knees. "Don't talk either, if you don't mind."

Maybe that would be better.

Maybe she'd close her eyes. She tried it, but the feeling of the cold lube and his finger rubbing it around — *inside* — was too much.

She opened her eyes instead, wanting something else to concentrate on. She turned her face to watch the smoke in the ashtray instead. It was curling up, one tiny white strand that dissipated into the air above. It was mesmerizing.

She didn't react to the feeling of him inside her.

She looked at the smoke instead.

And then it was just happening.

I'm being raped, she thought, staring at the smoke. *And it's not actually that bad. I can deal with this.*

She almost laughed at the absurdity of it.

But it was true as far as that went, she supposed. It didn't hurt. The lube had taken care of any true discomfort. Obviously, it was invasive, but it was bearable. It didn't feel good, but then she pretty much never thought penetration felt like much of anything.

One more reason she'd convinced herself she must be a man when she was a teenager. Sex felt like nothing to her. She had one boyfriend before Carter with whom she'd attempted it a few times, the only guy she'd ever dated as a woman, unless Liam counted, which…

We were going to have a baby together. That must mean it counts.

But they'd never said that to each other, called each other boyfriend or girlfriend, made it into a thing.

No, don't think about Liam.

Right, not Liam, because it was probably the only time she'd had penetrative sex with any regularity — vaginal penetrative sex — and the only time she'd ever much enjoyed it, and that was mostly because of her own insistence on her clitoris being stimulated.

When she'd been with Carter, they'd just called it her dick. Or sometimes her guy-clit, which was a funny sort of secret thing between the two of them, and why was she thinking about this while all this was happening?

She tried to clear her mind and stare at the smoke.

Her mind wouldn't clear.

Carter hadn't been keen on using her vagina, because he was a gay man, and he wasn't attracted to such things, and she had said it was worthless because she was actually a man, and that there was no point in using it for sex because it did nothing for her, and the only time she and Carter ever really had sex that way was when she wasn't in the mood for being on the receiving end of anal and she convinced him to fuck her there instead — for convenience.

But it was just… just a hole, that's all. She'd done research on this since and discovered that not feeling anything during sex didn't mean she wasn't female. There just weren't very many actual nerve endings in the vagina, and the only way that vaginal penetration resulted in much sexual pleasure was from tugging on the clitoris, and apparently women were all shaped differently and some got more tugging than others, and she was one of the ones who got very little.

Thank God, she thought, almost laughing again.

Because if it had felt good, it would have been worse.

This was just… nothing.

It was like the sex she'd had as a teenager, the sex she'd consented to, the sex that had been boring and awkward as she lay there while her then-boyfriend had sex on her —

I'm not being raped, Finn is just having sex on me.

In me.

She didn't want to think about this anymore. She didn't want to think anything, as a matter of fact.

How much longer could this go on?

She moved her head to look at him.

He slapped her face back the way it had been, and that stung, and she whimpered.

"Fuck, Haysle, no noises," he growled. "And *don't* move."

The pain was like a thousand tiny bright needles on her face, on her jaw, on her cheekbone. Her teeth ached. Tears came to her eyes, but she didn't blink or acknowledge them, she just lay there, boneless.

The pain helped.

She could focus on the pain and then she didn't have to think, and she didn't have to feel him in there, she could just feel the pain, the sting, and she clung to the sensation for as long as she could, even as it began to fade.

Luckily, he was done before it could fade entirely.

He pulled out of her and zipped up and climbed off the mattress and lit another cigarette. "Don't move yet," he told her, his voice scratchy.

She didn't.

Her legs were shaking.

That happened sometimes when she had sex like this. It happened with Liam.

Don't think about Liam.

Liam was having sex with Destiny to save her, and that was just like Liam to do something stupid like that, to sacrifice himself, and she *hated* that.

The leg-shaking thing, she thought it must have something to do with some muscles that were used in the whole process, but she hadn't thought she was using any muscles, because she had been just lying there and she hadn't responded, so maybe there was some other reason why the shaking happened.

But she couldn't stop it, even though she tried to, and she tensed, waiting for Finn to notice —

It was insidious that she couldn't even call him Slater anymore, that it was all intimate between them, *fuck* him —

To notice and then hit her again.

But he just smoked and didn't look at her.

Eventually, he came over and smashed the cigarette butt next to the other one, which had finally gone out. Now there was another thread of smoke to stare at, because she hadn't moved.

He picked up her pajamas and underwear and put them on her belly in a crumpled heap. He gazed down at her.

Still, she didn't move.

"I don't think you'll see Liam," he said finally. "But if you do, it would be a bad idea to tell him I did this to you. He wouldn't like it."

The laugh burst out of her, wild and uncontrolled. Suddenly, she was moving —*fuck* him —and she yanked on her clothes and shook all over and clenched her hands into fists and then was pistoning up off the bed to advance on him, and she was nothing but rage.

Why was this happening now?

Why not before?

Why not when she could have stopped him —

Hadn't she decided not to do that, that there was no way to get free?

She shoved him, hands on his chest.

He took two steps back, absorbing the impact. He blinked at her.

"You're going to be recaptured and taken back to jail and they're going to give you a lethal injection, and on that day, I'm going to be there," she said, breathless. "I'm going to be there, and I'm going to laugh, and the last sound you will hear on this earth will be my laughter as you are descending into *hell*."

She stalked around him and to the stairs, which she began clambering down, her breath coming in noisy gasps.

"So, it wasn't good for you?" he called after her.

She let out a string of barely audible swears as she went even faster.

But he caught up with her on the second floor. He took her by the wrist.

She tried to pull her hand away.

He tightened his grip to a painful crush.

She let out a breathy high-pitched protest.

"Hey, what are you doing?" he said in a harsh whisper.

"Going back to bed," she spat at him.

He let go of her. "I'll walk you there."

"You don't need to," she said.

"I will, though," he said. "And you won't try to escape again."

"Or this will happen again?" Why did she sound like she might cry?

"I can make it a lot worse." This was matter-of-fact. "And if Destiny finds out… well, you don't want her to find out."

She turned on her heel and stalked away from him.

He went two paces behind her all the way back to her room.

He stood in the doorway while she climbed up into her bunk.

She lay there, feeling his semen leak out of her and clenching her hands into fists and releasing them while he *stayed* in the goddamn doorway. Every time she opened her eyes, he was there, until the time she opened her eyes and it was morning.

CHAPTER FOUR

SHE DIDN'T SEE Slater again, not for over a week.

She wouldn't have known it was a week, except she counted the days. She got confused sometimes, and she couldn't remember if it was two days since the rape or three days, but she settled on two days, since it seemed better to undercount than overcount.

During that week, she did her chores and her meditation drills and she was quiet and meek and she didn't even think about escape.

That wasn't true.

She did think about it.

But when she did, she only felt a dull ache of despair, because she was never going to be able to escape.

The day she saw Slater again, she was in the kitchen, making breakfast, and he came over to her while she was making pancakes. He touched her.

He touched her all over and it made her skin crawl. He rubbed his big hand over her, down to rest, splayed out, on the small of her back as he surveyed the pancakes.

She wanted to tell them to go away, that he was making her nervous, but she felt as if she'd give him power over her if he knew he unnerved her, and he already had too much power over her.

He moved his hand and tucked a strand of her hair behind her ear.

She flinched and flipped all the pancakes too soon, sending pancake batter to splatter out in long bursts as each pancake wetly hit the sizzling pan.

He rubbed her facial hair.

Her nostrils flared.

"You want some avocado toast?" he said softly.

"No," she said tightly.

He just laughed. He pressed his mouth into her temple.

She shuddered.

"Good girl, Haysle," he breathed. "We're almost ready." Then he was gone.

Almost ready for what?

She remembered he'd said something about how she could go home and that he and Liam were working on it. She turned to look after him and she wondered what deals with the devil that Liam was making and she felt vaguely ashamed of herself for not holding up better.

Liam had been raped by Finn, too.

Liam wasn't falling the fuck apart.

She turned back to the skillet grimly.

DESTINY WAS SITTING at a huge, oaken desk, in a room lined with bookshelves. There were books stacked on the desk too, and Haysle cocked her head to read the titles of them. It was a stack of books written by Samson Black, and Haysle had heard of them. They were true crime narratives, but the guy who wrote them always seemed to insert himself into the narrative in some way. She even thought there had been some scandal lately, lots of the women coming out on Twitter to claim he had coerced them into sexual relationships.

Destiny reached across and picked up *Little Girl Lost.* "Have you read it?"

Haysle shook her head. What was she doing here?

"It's fascinating really," said Destiny. "This man, this writer, Samson Black, he twists himself up in knots to try to convince himself that Lola Ward is just a helpless victim." She handed the book over to Haysle.

"Lola," said Haysle, furrowing her brow. "Is that why you went by Lola?" Destiny had used the name Lola as a screen name for her fanfic, and she'd also been called Lola by the original permutation of her cult, back when she was in college and she used to host bonfires.

"I thought no one was ever going to get the reference," said Destiny. "But I guess I did have to feed it to you."

"You don't think she was a victim?" said Haysle. She barely remembered the case, but she thought that Lola Ward had been twelve when she'd been seduced by some man in his twenties or something who'd then killed her parents and abducted her along on a murder spree. His defense had been that Lola had *made* him do it.

Destiny shrugged.

"You think the little girl masterminded it all?" said Haysle.

"Some parents need killing," said Destiny.

"Like your father?" said Haysle.

"Are you interrogating me?" said Destiny. "Are you still playing detective? I told Finn you wouldn't be so easily cowed. He doesn't think very highly of women, I'm afraid."

Haysle let out a snort.

"As it happens, I might want you to play detective," said Destiny. "Talk to me about Liam?"

"What about Liam?"

"Do you really believe him when he pretends he didn't know about all this?" Destiny gestured around. "You saw that video I sent you, didn't you? The one with Cora? What did he tell you about that?"

Haysle folded her arms over her chest. "Why don't we skip that part and go straight to the part where you tell me what you *want* me to think about the video."

Destiny just laughed. "All right. But it's the truth, Haysle, not what I want you to think. Liam and Finn killed Cora together. Liam has been helping Finn kill all along."

Haysle let out a guffaw. "Don't be ridiculous."

"Come *on*, Haysle," said Destiny. "You really think they were just both obliviously *both* living in Cape Christopher for all that time?"

Haysle'd had this thought before. "I already suspected him. I'm not… we're not doing that again."

The escape plot happened already, whispered Liam's voice in her brain.

"Back then, they both thought I was dead," said Destiny, "and doing Cora together was their homage to that first experience together. I didn't send you that part of the video."

Haysle just blinked at her.

Destiny smiled. "Maybe if I let you go, I will. But if I do, will you send Liam to jail or will you cover up his sins?"

"Let me go…?" Haysle eyed Destiny warily.

"Well, you can't go now," said Destiny. "Not quite yet. We'll do a few sessions together, I think, and then you might be ready." She made a tent with her fingers and settled them against her chin. "Liam is willing to do all sorts of things for you. It'll be interesting to see what you're willing to do for him."

"I really don't understand—"

"Ricardo!" Destiny's suddenly threw back her head and bellowed.

The door to the study opened, and Haysle turned to see that Ricky Hernandez was standing there. He'd been captured by Destiny before all this started. They'd been doing this to get Ricky back.

Ricky's gaze slid over her, but he didn't seem to recognize her. "Yes, my queen?" he said to Destiny.

Destiny tilted her head. "There are purple flowers on the meadow, Ricardo. It's time to pluck them."

Ricky blinked hard and then he ran over to Haysle's chair, skidding to his knees next to her. "Haysle, it's you? Haysle, did he get to you?"

Haysle pulled away, disliking everything about this, feeling out of sorts and off balance. "Who?"

"Liam, of course," said Ricky.

"Ricardo, there is a calm ocean," said Destiny. "The waves are smoothed away."

Ricky immediately got to his feet, blank and blinking, like an automaton. "Yes, my queen?"

She did some hypnosis on me, and my addiction just went away, came the echo of Monique's voice.

Haysle shrank back into her chair, swallowing hard.

Destiny got up from her desk and swept across the room. She went out the doorway into the hall, not looking back at them, just beckoning with one hand. "Follow me," she sang.

Ricky went after her immediately, and Haysle got up and brought up the rear.

They went downstairs and out onto the porch. A car had been pulled up to the front porch. Tyler was driving it.

"Goodbye, Ricardo," said Destiny, running her fingers over Ricky's face. "Do the right thing when you get free."

Ricky smiled at Destiny. "I will, my queen." He bowed to her, bending at the waist, eyes on her like an adoring puppy. Then he went to the car, opened the door, and slid inside.

The car drove off down the driveway.

Destiny leaned in close. "There he goes, Haysle. Would you like that to be you someday?"

Haysle turned to look at her. "You're just letting him go?" Then she shook her head. "No, you got into his head. You broke into his brain, and you played around in there, and you want to do that to me, too."

"I want to help you, Haysle," said Destiny, clucking her tongue in gentle admonition. "But not if you're not ready."

"Ready for a hypnosis session?" Haysle's voice was tight. "No, thank you."

Destiny shrugged. "All right, well, I can wait." She turned and went back into the house, leaving Haysle alone on the porch.

Haysle stared into the wake of the car, thinking of how impossible escape was, thinking of how long it would be until that hypnosis session sounded pretty good to her.

CHAPTER FIVE

WHEN HAYSLE WOKE in the night, she thought it was another meditation drill, but instead it was Finn at the foot of her bunk bed, tugging on her ankle, whispering for her to get up.

She sat up and looked down at him.

What was he going to do to her now?

"Haysle," came a voice from the doorway.

She looked up to see Liam there, shirtless, his chest smeared with something red which was clumped in his chest hair. Now, looking back at Finn, she realized there was a fine spray of red all over his chin and cheek.

"Come on," said Finn.

But beneath her bunk, Monique was stirring. "What's going on?" she said in a normal voice. The other girls were stirring too.

"Don't, Monique," said Finn, yanking something out from his belt.

It was a big kitchen knife, and it was bloody.

Finn pointed the tip at Monique.

Haysle let out noisy gasps.

"Haysle." Liam beckoned from the doorway.

"What did you guys do?" she breathed.

"Ding dong, the bitch is dead," said Finn with a wide, awful grin. "Now, come on."

Monique moved toward Finn.

He moved quickly, grabbing her around the shoulders and turning her.

The knife slicked into her skull.

Haysle screamed.

"For fuck's sake, Finn," said Liam, annoyed.

Finn pulled the knife out and Monique's body slid lifeless to the floor. "Sorry."

"You know, the thing is, you're not," said Liam. "*Haysle.*"

She shook her head.

Finn reached up. "I'll help you down.

"Don't *touch* me," she snarled at him, kicking with her feet.

"What's that about?" said Liam.

"We have a deal, Liam," said Finn in a silky voice, "and if you—"

"Move," Haysle said to Finn in a tight voice.

Finn backed up.

Haysle turned and climbed out of the bunk bed. She shot a glance at Kyleigh and Pam who were cowering in their beds. She turned away from them and picked up her boots. "So, you killed Destiny?"

"I..." Liam wouldn't meet her gaze. "We did it together."

Haysle stepped into her boots, tying them up. "I seem to remember this was what you wanted when you captured us and took us to that beach house, Finn." She looked at Liam. "You gave him what he *wanted.*"

"Since when do you call him Finn?" said Liam, leveling his gaze at her.

"Let's go," said Finn, hauling Haysle up from the crouch she'd gotten in to tie her boots. He nudged her forward, and she hurried away from him.

She collided with Liam, and he recoiled from her touch, and she started to back away from him.

But then he grabbed her and pulled her against him, resting his forehead against hers, one hand rubbing up and down her upper arm. "Hey," he breathed. "Hey."

A lump rose in her throat. "Hey," she whispered.

"This is sweet," snapped Finn. "Let's go."

Liam jerked away.

Finn led with the bloody knife.

Liam went after him, reaching back to lace his fingers with Haysle's, tugging her along with the both of them.

Finn ran the tip of the blade down the railing of the staircase, barely scratching it, leaving smears of blood in its wake.

Liam clutched her hand and they went down side by side, even though it was a little crowded next to each other because Liam's shoulders were so broad.

They stopped at the door and got jackets. Liam zipped up a hooded sweatshirt over his bare chest. She shrugged into a lined windbreaker. Finn yanked a pullover over his head.

Finn opened the door.

"You're sure he's gone?" said Liam.

"I told you, yes," said Finn, annoyed.

"Who?" said Haysle.

"Ricky Hernandez," said Liam, looking down on her.

"I watched him go," said Haysle. "She did something to him."

"It's what she does," said Finn, almost rueful. He was out on the porch. "Did. What she *did*."

Liam went out after him, and Haysle was still linked to him, so she went too.

They didn't walk down the driveway, though. Instead, Finn led them across to a detached garage. It was open and a car was parked inside.

Finn pulled a set of keys out of his pocket and the car beeped, headlights flashing, as he unlocked it.

Haysle pressed into Liam. "Why are we taking him with us?" she whispered.

Liam glanced at her. "I…"

"He…" The words were stuck in her throat. She couldn't say the damned word aloud. "Forced himself."

Liam stiffened.

"On me," she finished, and now her voice was louder.

Liam let go of her and took two steps to close the distance between him and Finn. He slammed his hand into the back of the other man's head.

Finn grunted, staggering away, clutching the back of his skull and turning on Liam with fury.

"Fuck you," said Liam. "*Fuck* you."

"What the hell? What was that for?" Finn was all wounded innocence.

Liam's voice was scoured. "I said, and I remember this specifically, 'Hands off Haysle, no one touches Haysle,' and you said—"

"She tried to run," said Finn.

Liam turned to her. "Did you?"

"She must have made it all the way to the fence, because Mick was bringing her back when I saw them both," said Finn. "She was going to fuck everything up, and I had to make her compliant, and it worked, so I'm sorry if you're not willing to do the things that need to be done, but I am, and—"

"Why didn't you just tell her to lay low, and that we were working on it?" said Liam.

"He did," whispered Haysle. "He did, but…"

"We don't have time for this right now," said Finn.

"No, I guess not," said Liam. He stalked over to the car and opened the back door. He gestured. "Get in, Haysle."

"With him?" she said.

Liam wouldn't meet her gaze.

"What is going on, Liam?" said Haysle.

"He and I have a deal," said Liam. He lifted his gaze to Finn. "Although, in point of fact, you did already break the terms."

"Oh, I'm sorry," said Finn. "Leave me behind, then. Would *you* like to stab whoever's on the gate? I think it's Jennifer tonight. You ready to cut another woman tonight?"

"*Fuck.*" Liam threw up both of his hands.

Haysle scurried over and got into the back seat.

Liam scooted in next to her. He yanked the door shut and buried his face in his hands.

Finn got into the front seat and fitted the key to the ignition.

Liam lifted his face, and his cheeks were wet. He was shaking.

The car sped down the driveway until they came to the gate. Finn pulled it to a stop and rolled down the window.

Jennifer came over, leaning into the car. "I didn't get authorization on this, Phineas. What's going on?"

Finn brought the knife up under her chin.

Her eyes went wide in fear and pain and then blank.

Finn pulled the knife back out and Jennifer's body thudded against the ground. Finn turned to look at Liam. "I guess you're going to want me to get the key off her body, too?"

II: LIAM EMERSON

CHAPTER SIX

LIAM HAD A bag over his head and he was prodded out of the back seat of the car by a gun against his ribs. He didn't know where Haysle was, and he yelled for her, but Tyler's voice growled for both of them to shut up.

They had just been captured, and they'd spent a long car ride with Finn in the back seat. Liam was fairly sure they were being taken to Destiny. This must be her hideout, such as it was.

Liam was trying to calculate where they could be, but he was limited to his own perception of how long they had traveled, and he didn't really have any idea how long they'd driven. He thought it had been hours. Two hours, maybe? Three? That was a wide radius around Cape Christopher.

He should have paid attention to the position of the sun before they put the bag over his head.

No, he had… It had been against his left cheek. He'd been able to see the light through the bag, been able to feel the heat.

So, um, that would mean that west was to his left, so they'd been traveling north.

Right?

North or maybe northwest. They couldn't really have gone northeast or they would have been in the ocean.

Did it help, though?

And while he was thinking this, he was being forced to

walk, and he was stumbling up a set of stairs onto a porch and then into a house, and then up another set of stairs.

He was urged into a room and Tyler yanked his arms above his head and handcuffed him and then hooked him into something, stretching him out, hanging him there.

Then he was left alone.

He was left alone in the room, with his hands cuffed and his arms hooked into something in the ceiling, until it was dark.

Finally, someone yanked the bag off his head.

Destiny was there, right below him, peering up at him, looking the same but older, more lines on that face of hers, and her makeup settling into those creases around her eyes.

"I need to take a piss," he said.

She laughed. "Of course." She left the room and came back with a bucket, which she set in front of him.

He glared at her.

She smiled. "Not good enough for you?"

"I… my pants…"

"Right." So, of course, she took them off entirely.

And then his bladder was empty but he was naked from the waist down and the room was cold and she left him there.

She left him there for two days, and she didn't feed him or give him water, and the handcuffs chafed and his hands were numb and when she came back and said she'd let him down and give him some water but he had to do exactly as she said, he agreed immediately.

The water tasted like life itself.

He'd never tasted anything so good.

He lulled on the floor—still half naked, leaning against the wall, holding a cup with a straw in it that he sipped from carefully, because the water was good but his body wasn't used to it and he needed to go slow.

It felt like a hangover, like after drinking too much, only multiplied by ten thousand.

His head was pounding, and it seemed to hurt worse as he drank, even though he knew that didn't make any sense.

"Liam." Her voice was soothing and soft and comforting. "Look at me."

He did.

"I want you to imagine yourself in a warm, safe place, can you do that?"

He nodded.

"Close your eyes?" she murmured.

He closed his eyes. He was tired. He had slept, but not well, not when he'd been suspended from the ceiling.

"Tell me about where you are," she said.

"I'm…" He sighed. "Home. Belinda is downstairs making breakfast, but I'm still half asleep in bed." He knew this wasn't right, that Belinda wasn't his wife and that house where he'd lived was no longer his home, but that was what he'd conjured, and he leaned into it.

"Good," said the voice, which now sounded like Belinda's voice. "In that place between waking and dreaming, where everything is muted and soft around the edges?"

"Yes," he said, and he spread out the last 'S' sound, making it almost a hiss.

"Stay there," said the Belinda-like voice. "Stay *here*. Is it good here?"

"Uh huh."

"You like it here, and you'll come back here whenever you need to, all right? I'll tell you to picture the bed and the smells of breakfast and you'll be right here, Liam. *Right* here, very safe."

He sighed again.

CHAPTER SEVEN

LIAM JERKED AWAKE standing in an unfamiliar room filled with exercise equipment. He was wearing pants now. He had no idea how he'd gotten here or where these pants had even come from. He ran his fingers over them and looked around the room.

There was an ancient treadmill, so old that it couldn't possibly work anymore, and two exercise bikes and a rowing machine. The rowing machine looked new. The floor was hardwood—old and dark and scuffed a bit, a little warped in the way that old flooring was. From the look of the walls and the doorway and the windows, this was an old house.

He lurched toward the door of the room and stepped out into the hallway.

Finn was lounging next to the door, wearing a tight white tank top that clung to his chest and abdomen, and he looked good. "Hey, tiger."

Liam swallowed. "What's going on?"

"You hungry?"

He was starving. He nodded dumbly.

Finn pushed off the wall, gesturing with his head. "This way." He started down the hallway.

Liam followed him.

Finn talked as they walked. "It's a little far out for fast food, unfortunately. No deliveries out in the middle of nowhere, you know. No Doordash, no Grubhub, no Ubereats. Nada. And it's too far to drive and pick it up myself, even if I had car privileges, which I don't." He glanced over his shoulder. "She doesn't trust me."

"You mean Destiny?"

They emerged into a kitchen, and Liam looked around at its size and scope. It looked like a place fit to feed an army. Of course, Destiny did have a cult, didn't she?

"And," Finn continued, going over to the refrigerator, "I'm not really much for cooking." He bent down to open the freezer, which was one of those drawers on the bottom. He sorted through and came out with a bag of pasta, one of those meals for two that Liam could always easily eat by himself, this one with shrimp and cream sauce and peas. His stomach growled. Finn set it on the counter. "This, I can do, though. Will you eat this for me, tiger?"

"Definitely," said Liam, who didn't care if Finn watched, because he was too hungry to care.

Finn crossed the kitchen and touched Liam. He ran his fingertips over Liam's jaw and his neck.

Liam self-consciously realized he needed to shave as Finn's fingers tickled his facial hair.

"Good," said Finn in a low, throaty voice.

"I'm really hungry, Finn," said Liam. "Can we skip this?"

Finn threw back his head and laughed.

IT WASN'T UNTIL he was halfway into the bowl of pasta—he had not been given the entire bag either, but had to share halfsies with Finn, even though Finn wasn't eating but simply greedily watching Liam eat—that Liam remembered Haysle.

He hated himself for that.

"Where's Haysle?" What the fuck was wrong with him? How could he not have asked about her first thing? The woman could very possibly be carrying his child, after all. He was a piece of *shit*.

"Haysle's in the hole," said Finn. "I'll show you what the rooms are like after you eat."

"Fuck that, show me now," said Liam, scooting out his chair and standing up.

"Eat, tiger," said Finn.

"No," said Liam, folding his arms over his chest. Piece of shit. Pregnant woman nowhere to be seen and Liam could only think about his own goddamned hunger. Why was he *such* a fuck-up?

Finn raised an eyebrow. "You leave that, you can't finish it."

"Fuck," said Liam, and—shamefully—picked up the bowl and the fork and shoveled almost all of what remained in the bowl into his mouth. He chewed, glaring at Finn.

Finn was glaring too. "That's not how you eat pasta, tiger. You should have savored that food, and I'm annoyed, because this is all she gave me, watching you eat, and…" He sighed heavily and got up from the table. "Well, come on."

They went into the basement, and it was dark down there and there were concrete rooms.

"I think she locked her in one of the bathrooms," said Finn, gesturing around at the empty room. "That Hernandez of yours, though—"

"Ricky's here?"

"Ricky's in the hole too," said Finn.

"Where?" said Liam, who felt even more guilty, because he'd forgotten all about Ricky again. And Ricky had gotten captured because the guy was hurt about how Liam had ended things between them.

I go around sticking my dick in people and then I don't do right by them, he thought.

"We can't get them out," said Finn. "I don't have key clearance. Tyler has key clearance, but not me. I'm working on it, but she…" He made a face. "She can be really frustrating, you know. I think she likes me better than someone as malleable as Tyler. I'm more exciting, because I'm unpredictable. That turns her on, but… well, like I said, she doesn't trust me. She wants you to know they're down here, though. She wants you to know she has leverage."

Liam blinked. "So, she wants to use that against me, the knowledge that people I care about are suffering?"

"You're weak in that way, tiger," said Finn with a shrug.

Liam clenched his hands in fists. "What's she want from me?"

"She wants to watch us fuck," said Finn. "That was the lure, wasn't it? You set that all up hoping she'd come and try to watch us making her a little porno."

Right. It was true. Destiny had sent demands to Haysle, saying that if she was given a film of Finn and Liam together, she'd release Ricky. But they hadn't done it, and now they'd all been captured.

It shouldn't surprise him that Destiny was just that serious about it all.

"Well, so, what?" Liam let his shoulders sag. "I bend over for you and she lets them out?"

"Come on, Liam, don't be an idiot," said Finn. "We're not caving to her."

"*What?*" Liam's eyes widened. "*You're* refusing?"

"I am not her masturbatory toy," said Finn, lifting his chin, looking incensed. "She doesn't respect me. She doesn't get to control me. I don't just wind up and do tricks."

Liam thought Finn was mixing metaphors there, but he decided not to point that out. "Finn, Haysle, she…" He drew in a breath. "She might be pregnant. She can't be down here, okay? So, I need to get her out of here."

"Pregnant? She can get pregnant? I thought she was a man for half her life."

"Well, she was born female, and she didn't alter her body in such a way to prevent it. She's been off testosterone long enough that it's all practically reversed."

Finn ran a hand through his hair. "Shit. This is why you've been the way you've been. This is why you turned on me."

"Turned on you? What the fuck are you talking about?"

"She *took* you from me." Finn sounded genuinely anguished. "Of course you'd be swayed by the thought that your spawn was growing in her. Of course."

"Look, I am not yours. I have never been yours—"

"I'm yours, you fuckwad," said Finn, baring his teeth at Liam.

Liam backed away from this, unsettled by it. Also, he was actually still hungry and he felt a little lightheaded. That had not been very much food, not to make up for days with nothing.

"I'm not weak, never weak, except when it comes to you." Finn poked Liam in the middle of the chest.

Liam looked down at Finn's finger there, and it was on the tip of his tongue to tell Finn that was bullshit, because Finn didn't care about Liam. Finn used Liam. Finn raped Liam. Finn tried to frame Liam for murder. Finn captured Liam and hurt him and abused him.

But, well, Finn was also psychotic, and maybe it was useful if Finn thought he cared about Liam. Maybe that was not a bubble he should burst, not in a delicate situation like this.

So, Liam simply wrapped his hand around Finn's and picked it up and carefully brought his fingers to his mouth. "Okay," he said. He pressed his lips into Finn's knuckles. "Well, I appreciate that."

"Do you?" Finn's voice was husky. "Do you really? Or are you just playing me? When I was locked up, you came in there and told me that no one cared if I lived or died, that I wasn't a person."

"That was—"

"It was her. Detective fucking Dawson," Finn sneered. "She poisoned you against me."

"No," said Liam, shaking his head, because he did not want Finn to hate Haysle, because Finn might hurt Haysle if he hated her. "No, it wasn't her, I swear. It was just, um, just..." He kissed another of Finn's knuckle, catching the other man's eye. "Sometimes, you gotta let me top you is all, huh? It's just... just a little game. You don't always get to make me submit, sometimes it's hot for you to—"

"I do not kink that way," said Finn tightly.

"Sorry." Liam kissed another knuckle. "I'll never try it again."

Finn snatched his hand back. "You're... you're..." He rubbed his knuckles, looking confused. "What are you doing?"

"Nothing," said Liam. "How do you get key clearance?"

"Of course it's about her," said Finn.

"Hey," said Liam, reaching out for the other man. He snatched Finn's chin and made him look at him. "Have we known each other a long time?"

"You know we have," said Finn warily.

"Am I the first man you ever kissed?"

"Why are you—"

"Do you really think I could replace you with a *woman?*"

"She's sort of half-dude," said Finn in a sulky voice.

"No, she's not," said Liam.

Finn ducked backward, getting out of Liam's touch. "Destiny doesn't trust me, and I can't trust you. We're in a pretty fucked up situation here, tiger."

"Why can't you trust me?" said Liam.

Finn turned his back on him and stalked away, off into the shadows of the basement.

"Finn!" Liam went after him.

But he didn't know what happened. Maybe Finn disappeared into one of the dark rooms with open doors, rooms that Liam walked past. He must have, because Liam never caught up with him, and when he climbed to the top of the steps, Finn was nowhere to be seen.

Liam took the opportunity to go back to the dining room table and eat the remaining pasta in both his bowl and Finn's, even though the woman who'd captured them came in—Monique was her name, he remembered—and said that she needed the dishes. He upended the bowl into his mouth and swallowed the last of it before handing it over.

"Where's Destiny?" he asked Monique.

"I don't know," said Monique.

So, Liam went looking for her.

He searched the whole house, and he discovered that part

of the house was in pretty bad shape. He didn't know if there had been a burst pipe or a leak or a broken bathtub, but there was serious water damage on a set of rooms all stacked on top of each other, from the top floor down, and there were three stories. Black mold was creeping up over the paint, and the wallpaper was rotting off the walls.

Seemed like Destiny's kind of place.

She liked places that were falling apart.

But eventually he found her in a bookshelf-lined room, which was in fine condition and even had a working fireplace, where a cheerily dancing fire was burning.

"Why isn't Finn with you?" she said.

"I don't know. He disappeared," said Liam. "I want Haysle out of there."

"Didn't Finn tell you what I want?" she said.

"I'm fine with it," said Liam. "He's not."

She furrowed her brow. "He's pissed at me," she said thoughtfully.

"Come on, is there something else I can do?" he said, spreading his hands. "Something else you want? Some way I can get Haysle out? And Ricky too." *Fuck, why do I always forget about Ricky?*

Destiny went over to a big oak desk and trailed her fingers over several stacks of books on it.

"Why'd you capture us anyway? How do you think this ends? They work for the fucking police. You think you're clever, but this is a whole department of law enforcement who are primed to protect their own, and if you—"

"It was you, at first." She looked up at him. "You were sweet, Liam. I wanted to want a sweet guy like you. I really did."

"You don't want me?" He took a step toward her. "Why am I here?"

"You were just too easy to control. And too sweet. You wouldn't even get angry. I was pretty much the worst girlfriend in the history of the world. I cheated on you constantly, and you just didn't… did you not notice?"

"You said my jealousy was boring."

"And then you stopped being jealous." She let out a little laugh as if she couldn't belief that. "You're just... highly suggestible, Liam."

"I didn't stop being jealous," he said. "I stopped telling you about it, that's all."

She eyed him. "Why?"

"Because I guess I wanted us to keep fucking?"

"Why not just fuck someone else?"

"It's not like I didn't," he muttered.

She drew back. "Really?"

"I mean, freshman year, when it all started with you and me, and you were all, 'No fucking anyone else, including Finn'? No, not then. But then we were apart for long periods of time—"

"Well, that's not the same thing."

"Even when we were technically together, I just figured we weren't being exclusive," he said.

"Oh," she said, eyeing him, surprised. "Well. I wouldn't have expected that. I guess I wasn't paying much attention to you, then, though, because it wasn't you anymore. It was him."

"Is this supposed to make me jealous now?" he muttered. "If you want Finn, I'm fine with it." He cringed. "Wait, is he listening right now, because—"

"He's the only person I've ever met who *isn't* highly suggestible," she said. "He's... I can't control him. I don't even want to control him. If I could control him, I wouldn't want him, do you understand?"

"You know, I don't. I don't attempt to control people myself, so—"

"Bullshit, everyone tries to control other people. The difference is that most people can't handle the truth of themselves and they need to pretend they have morals. It gets in their way of achieving what it is they want."

"But it's ultimately meaningless when they get it," he said. "Because, once you control something, it's worthless, and you don't even want it anymore."

She made a sour face at him. "Why don't you shut your

mouth, hmm?"

"Struck a nerve?" he said, raising his eyebrows.

"I thought you came here to beg for your girlfriend." She folded her arms over her chest. "This doesn't sound like begging."

"I came to bargain," he said. "That's how Finn made it sound. I give Finn my ass and in return Haysle and Ricky are free. Is that not the offer?"

Her nostrils flared. "Maybe there is something you can do for me, Liam."

"I want your promise that—"

"No promises. Make me happy and I'll think about freeing Haysle."

"And Ricky."

"Ricky's almost ready to leave the hole on his own," she said. She pointed to a chair in front of her desk. "Sit down."

He sighed heavily and then came and sat down. "What am I doing here?"

"Close your eyes," she said, and the pitch of her voice had changed.

He glared at her.

"Liam," she said.

"Fine." He closed his eyes.

"There's a warm bed, and breakfast cooking downstairs," she said. "You're not quite awake and not quite aslee—"

LIAM WAS NAKED and strung up again, handcuffs digging into his wrists. There was a bright light on the floor, like a work light used in home improvement, shining right into his eyes, making him cringe.

Finn was on his knees in front of him, and his mouth was on Liam's very hard cock.

Liam shuddered, trying to angle his hips away, trying to get his sense of equilibrium.

How did I get here?

"Relax," came Destiny's voice, floating out from the

darkness somewhere, beyond the other side of the bright light.

Finn's hand went around him, cupping one of his ass cheeks, holding him in place.

Liam thought about kicking Finn. Driving his bare foot into Finn's chest, kicking his tight, white tank top. *We used to call those wife-beaters in high school,* he thought nonsensically. He looked down at Finn. "I thought you weren't her masturbatory tool."

Finn rocked back, releasing Liam's glistening cock. "Just wanted to taste you, tiger."

"Fuck that, you've never sucked my dick."

"Haven't I?" Finn's tongue dragged over Liam's scrotum.

An involuntary shudder went through Liam.

Kick him.

Suddenly, there were hands behind him, Destiny's hands, reaching around, dragging her nails lightly over his rib cage, over his chest.

Liam let out a throaty cry.

"Make me happy," said Destiny's voice. "Remember our bargain."

"You said no promises," said Liam, but he stopped thinking about kicking Finn and instead switched tactics. There was a way to make this blow job end, and it was to come, and this was a shitty, awful situation, but any man on earth could come fast if he needed to, and Liam had his own pet fantasies.

It was only that they were...

He liked to pretend degrading things, because the thoughts turned him on, and this—*actual* degradation—was the antithesis of sexy, and yet...

It took him forty seconds tops.

Finn made a noise of protest and and then backed off, wiping his mouth. "Warn a guy, huh?"

Liam sagged against the chains, shuddering, feeling some stupid sense of power and realizing that it was false, because now they had his orgasm to hold over him, as if it meant he was somehow consenting.

He wanted to cry.
Couldn't do that.
Definitely couldn't—
His throat hurt when he breathed. His eyes stung.
Fuck.

CHAPTER EIGHT

LIAM WAS STILL naked, but the light was off. He was hanging there in the darkness and Finn was the only other person in the room, sitting over near one of the windows and smoking a cigarette.

The darkness in the room meant that Liam could see the outline of the windows, letting in a bit of moonlight. And he could see Finn's cherry, glowing, illuminating Finn's features faintly in red.

"What's she doing to me?" said Liam. "I'm losing time."

"I hate her," said Finn. "She's the reason I ended up in jail in the first place. She's a crazy bitch, you know that?"

Liam's hands were numb again, and his muscles ached. What day was it? How long had he been here? "Since when do you smoke? Destiny used to smoke."

"I'm stressed out lately," said Finn.

Liam let out a hollow laugh.

"You hate her too."

"Obviously, but if you hate her, you're doing a really funny job of showing it, aren't you?"

"I…" Finn stubbed out his cigarette. "I'm not really good at thinking things through. Like, thinking of things that could go wrong. I get ideas, and then I think they'll work, and usually they do, but when they don't, it takes me a while to adjust to the new reality."

"Okay, well, as fascinating as this is, is there some way

that maybe you can get me down?"

"I told you, I don't have key clearance."

"Great."

"See, when I was in jail, and you and Dawson came to me with that idea to go after Destiny, and then I had the chance to betray you guys and tell her, I figured it made better sense to go with her. Because you told me that I'll never get out of jail and that I can't be rehabilitated."

Liam sighed. Seriously? Did they have to go through this?

"But I didn't think it through. I thought, I'll get out, and I'll be free. But I forgot about what a bitch she is." Finn got up. He crossed the room to Liam.

Liam shied away from him instinctively, but he was bolted to the ceiling, so he wasn't going anywhere.

Finn wrapped an arm around his waist and hauled him up.

The tension on his wrists eased.

"Better?" murmured Finn, his face very close.

"Thanks," whispered Liam.

"Are you ready yet, tiger?"

Liam blinked at him. What the hell was he talking about? Then he knew.

This was what Finn had been taunting him about all along. He said that he'd been tormenting Liam all to try to get him "ready," because he wanted them to kill together, because Liam was what had been missing from his life. "You want us to kill her?" He barely whispered it.

"I told you I did before," said Finn. "I had a plan, and I have to admit that things went pretty pear-shaped, and this is not how I thought we'd get here, but…"

"Yes," said Liam.

"Good," said Finn. "Well, here's what we do. We say we're going to put on a little show for her, but then we get her in on it, just like before. She wants it. She wants us both."

"I think she wants you," said Liam. "She told me—"

"She knows that I want you," said Finn. "She wants me, I want you, you want… well, you'll pretend to want both of us."

"Okay," said Liam.

"We kill her while we're fucking her. Like before, only for real this time."

"Okay." Liam's voice broke.

Finn kissed him.

Liam kissed back, a kind of numb movement, instinctive, their tongues dancing.

Finn pulled back, making a harsh noise in the back of his throat. He pressed into Liam. He was hard.

Liam shuddered, feeling ill, feeling resigned, feeling—

"I can't just up and change my mind," said Finn. "She'll get suspicious."

"Oh, well, why didn't you—"

"I *told* you, I don't think things through so well." Finn's voice was fierce. "So, we have to ease into it. But this is how we get out of here."

"If you kill her, does that mean you get keys?"

"No," said Finn. "Shit."

"So, we have to get Destiny to let Haysle and Ricky out first."

"Because you're not going without them." Finn was annoyed but resigned.

"No." Liam just confirmed it. There was no point in getting angry at Finn at suggesting anything otherwise. Finn couldn't and didn't and wouldn't ever understand.

"That's good, that's good," said Finn. "It'll give us time to ease into it. I'll tell her... I'll start dropping hints about how much I think it would mean that you were softening up if you were willing to fuck her."

"Oh, by all means, whore me out."

"You're going to have to fuck her anyway when we kill her."

"Right." Liam sighed. "Fine."

"And then you tell her to let Dawson and Hernandez out if you do it."

"That's not going to work."

"It might. And once they're out, then I can start to soften her towards the idea of it and then we strike."

"Hey, Finn? Haysle gets out, no one's going to touch her, right? Hands off Haysle?"

"Oh, yeah, no worries. None of the women are allowed to fuck. Only the guys. Destiny makes them all do her, but otherwise, everyone's celibate. She'll be fine."

"Huh," said Liam. Kind of typical cult thing, wasn't it?

"All right," said Finn, letting out a breath. "All right."

"What's she *doing* to me, Finn? Why am I losing time?"

"It's the hypnotism thing, I guess," said Finn. "She started dabbling in it years ago. One of her pet projects, like how she always was, flitting from one thing to the next?"

Shit. He might have actually sort of let her in. But Liam had thought that hypnotism couldn't be forced on a person, that the person on the receiving end usually pushed back if the suggestions put in their brain were too extreme. He remembered reading that it was next to impossible to hypnotize someone into committing murder, so triggered sleeper assassins and the like were the purview of fiction.

So, Liam should be able to force her out the next time she tried it. He'd just have to be wary, and he couldn't let her back in.

Finn let him down so that he sagged against the cuffs again. "I have to go. I can't stay here with you. She has things she wants me to do and I need to make her think I'm softening towards her."

Liam nodded. "Yeah."

"If I could get you down—"

"It's okay."

"You know, I didn't know when I set this up that she was going to want to take you hostage too," said Finn. "If I'd known—"

"Don't," said Liam. "We both know it wouldn't have mattered."

Finn let out a little laugh. "Maybe it would have. I've never had a chance to prove myself to you, tiger." And with that, he was gone.

Liam glared after him.

He'd had only a *thousand* chances.

AND THEN TIME passed.

He hung from the ceiling and he thought about all the things that Finn had said and decided that none of it made sense, not really.

Finn said he didn't have key clearance and that he didn't have car clearance, but why couldn't Finn get those things?

Liam thought about it for thirty seconds and came up with a perfect plan. Finn had run of the house. Finn was not handcuffed and hung from the ceiling like a side of beef. Finn could go into the kitchen and get a knife. Finn was easily stronger than Destiny and would have no trouble being alone with her. Finn could overpower her, put the knife to her throat, and tell Tyler or whoever it was that had key and car privileges to hand these things over, and then Finn could convince Tyler to hand over a gun, because Tyler worshiped Destiny, and Tyler would do anything to save Destiny's life.

Yeah, if Finn wanted, they could get out of here easy.

And there was no reason to fuck Destiny to kill her.

She could be dead a number of other ways, easier ways.

In fact, killing her was probably stupid, because it was going to piss off Tyler and the others in the house, and Liam had already seen that Destiny's followers were ready and willing to commit violence in service of their wacko beliefs and their devotion to Destiny's mumbo jumbo.

So.

All of this?

Unnecessary.

Just Finn's way of manipulating him.

Finn wanted to make him kill.

It wasn't enough for Finn to rape his body and torture him.

No, Finn wanted his soul.

Liam could refuse. He could go back on all of it and tell Finn to fuck himself. He could demand they make a sane plan that didn't involve killing anyone or having sex with Destiny or any further disgusting and horrific compromises of his body and his mind.

If it was just me here, I would, he assured himself.

But there was Ricky, there was Haysle, there was the possibility of his baby. He...

I don't have a choice. Finn's got all the cards.

LIAM'S WRISTS WERE rubbed raw and bleeding, and his piss bucket was out of reach, and that was why he was yelling at the top of his lungs for some fucking help in here and had been for the past ten minutes.

Destiny appeared and crossed the room mutely. She was carrying a step stool with her, and she had to set that down to climb up and reach his cuffs. She unlocked them.

He collapsed, his entire body a series of aches and pains and agony.

Destiny got off the step stool and knelt next to him, her voice soft and soothing, and he *hated* that.

He vaulted up and staggered out of the room. He clutched the wall and stumbled down the hallway until he found a bathroom.

He sat down on the toilet to pee.

Fuck it.

Once his bladder was empty, he leaned sideways, resting his head and shoulder on the wall.

"Close your eyes, Liam," said Destiny in that soothing voice.

Resist, he urged himself. He did not close his eyes. Instead, he glared at her. "No more hypnosis."

She pressed her lips together in a firm line, not pleased.

He swallowed and held her gaze. "What are you trying to do to me? Do you really want to control me? What do you want me to do?"

She backed out of the doorway.

He groaned. His body still hurt, and he was exhausted

and hungry. He moved his head from the wall, but he felt dizzy.

No way could he stand up, at least not yet. He'd sit here for another minute, wait until he could get to his feet, and —

Destiny was back. She had clothes.

He tried to get up again.

The dizziness was so bad that he had to hold onto the wall for balance.

Destiny had to help him get dressed. Then she took him to the sink and opened the medicine cabinet and put antibiotic ointment on the scrapes on his wrists and bandaged them.

He felt grateful to her, because she was treating him with kindness now, and he knew that was bullshit.

But then there was food.

Not a lot of food. A bowl of rice with butter.

"You need something bland for your stomach right now," Destiny told him.

He thought what he probably needed was protein, but any food was good food, and he ate it quickly and then laid down in a bed, the bottom bunk in a room upstairs.

When he woke up, he was alone for the first time since he'd been in this place.

He was hungry again, but well rested, and he felt a bit stronger. He got up and went to look out the windows. He was on the second story. He couldn't jump from here. There didn't seem to be any handy drainpipes or trellises for him to climb up and down.

The door to his bedroom was open.

He went out into the hall.

There was no one there, but he could hear the sounds of people talking wafting up from the kitchen.

He went down the stairs and out the front door and stood on the porch, shivering and hugging himself. He was barefoot and wearing a t-shirt. It was cold enough outside that he could see his breath. He wasn't sure if it was morning or evening. The sun was gone but not the light, and the sky was gray.

Mist lay on the grass of the lawn.

Probably morning.

He should make a run for it. No one was watching him. He should run and try to get free, try to get to the main road, flag down a car, get on a cell phone, call for help.

I can't leave Haysle.

Right, but what good was he to her here? If he could get help, this ended. This nightmare, it was over.

I need shoes, he thought, looking down at his feet.

Did he? Did he really? Or was he just a pansy? A coward? Too soft to save his pregnant girlfriend?

Is she my girlfriend?

Fuck.

He went back inside. He told himself he was looking for shoes.

But Destiny was there, smiling at him. "You're awake. Come have breakfast."

CHAPTER NINE

DAYS PASSED.

LIAM wasn't sure how many, because sometimes, there was loud music in the night and he couldn't sleep and then Destiny would tell him to go down for a nap in the afternoon, and there was never enough food, and everything seemed unreal.

He didn't think he lost more time.

He didn't remember Destiny putting him into a hypnotic trance.

But he did go down for those naps without much of a fight.

Sometimes, she brought him back to her study and talked to him.

These didn't seem like hypnotic sessions, but then everything around him seemed a little hazy, and he felt weak and exhausted constantly.

He hadn't seen Finn since they'd made their little plan, and he hardly even remembered what he was supposed to be doing now. He did remember what Destiny had said about making her happy if he wanted Haysle to be free, and he vaguely thought there had been some discussion of his having sex with Destiny, but...

Did that even make sense?

Did Destiny even want to have sex with him?

And furthermore, why did Finn want him to have sex

with her?

"You miss Belinda, miss that marriage," said Destiny softly. "You couldn't do it, though, couldn't be the heterosexual husband and head of household. It's not in you, Liam. Even in that marriage, Belinda wore the pants."

Liam supposed this was supposed to make him angry or something. "Yes, let's be binary about it, shall we? If that's the case, Destiny, then you're a failed woman, right? You're just looking around for some man who's got it in him to dominate you. That's why you like Finn, because he's a wild card, and he frightens you, and it turns you on."

Destiny laughed. "Maybe."

"Or maybe you just want a man to be like your father," said Liam. "We did tests on Persephone, did you know that? We don't have your dad's DNA on file, but we're all ninety percent sure he's your daughter's father too."

Destiny laughed again.

"That's funny?" He leaned forward in his chair, adopting a nasty tone. "I guess you enjoyed it, then. I guess that was your idea of a great time."

Destiny didn't laugh again. She surveyed him. "You're really terrible at making me happy, Liam."

"What?" He shrugged. "This isn't making you find me more attractive? I'm just trying to be your type."

She raised her eyebrows. "Well." She got up from her desk and came over to him where he was sitting on the opposite side. She peered down at him, waiting.

He looked up at her.

They just gazed at each other for several long moments before he finally realized what she wanted.

Right.

Everything was hazy.

He was weak.

He reached up with trembling hands—*why are my stupid hands shaking*—and unbuttoned her pants. He unzipped them. He slid his hand inside, gliding over her silky underwear, rubbing her through the fabric.

It had been a while, but Destiny was the first girl he'd

ever gotten off, and she'd been pretty vocal about what she did and didn't like, something he'd actually appreciated, something he'd tried to cultivate in his later, shyer partners, wanting that explicit directive from sex, finding it *such* a turn-on. So, he knew his way around her here. He knew what he was doing.

And this was gross, because this was turning him on too.

Fuck.

With Finn, with the blow job, that had been one thing, because he could get himself off quickly, but getting a woman off quickly, that... yeah, that wasn't easy, and he wasn't at his best right now, not even close, and his hands were shaking.

He tried to look away, but she reached down and seized his chin and forced his gaze back up.

He rubbed her and he had to look into her eyes while he did it.

She said gross things, urging him on, praising him, calling him a good boy, other stuff that made him feel ill and also made him hard, and he wanted this over—*can it be over now*—but it wasn't. It went on and on, and her panties were wet and his fingers had a cramp, and then she was straddling him in that chair, and he was inside her, and she was touching herself now, which was better—no, not better, because now he was joined to her, and they were connected like this, and fuck, he still had to look into her eyes, she kept making him do that, and—

"I want you to go back to the bedroom, Liam, back to that warm liminal place between waking and sleeping, go back to that safe place, Liam, can you do that for me?"

Resist.

The rhythmic slap of their bodies, the tightness in his balls.

"Close your eyes, Liam."

HE WAS ON the porch, and Destiny was on the porch

swing.

"I'm letting her out," said Destiny.

He blinked at her. *How did I get here? What day is it?*

"You say one word to her, and I will put her back in there," said Destiny. "Do you understand me?"

He looked down at his hands. He turned them over and inspected them and there were no bandages and his wrists were healed and then he reached up and scratched at his chin. More growth there. *What day is it? How long have I been here?*

"Liam, do you understand?"

"Who?" he said.

"Haysle, of course," she said.

"Haysle," he said.

"I said to make me happy," said Destiny.

He licked his lips. "Did I?"

Destiny smiled.

"Good," he said.

"Don't talk to her," said Destiny. "And when you see her, you go inside, got it?"

He just stared. Haysle. Haysle and maybe the baby. If… if there was… she had said she had a negative pregnancy test, but she hadn't gotten her period, and there was a chance, there was still a chance…

"Liam," she snapped.

"Got it," he said.

Then it was quiet for a long, long time.

When Haysle eventually appeared, she hardly looked like herself. Her eyes were too big for her face, and the bones of her cheeks were too prominent. She looked at him, and he saw the spark of recognition in her face, but he looked away and went inside, just like Destiny had told him to.

He hovered, listening to their conversation. Haysle's voice was deep compared to Destiny's higher one, and whatever had been done to Haysle had made her voice deeper still.

"I want my tampons back," she said.

So.

No baby, then.

That was good.

That was better.

He was relieved.

He moved through the house, then, wandering aimlessly. He came into the dining room and Ricky was there, dressed and clean and shaved. He looked… good.

Liam had a flood of memories, all assaulting him at once. The first time he'd gone down on Ricky outside that bar, the way Ricky would always wake up in the morning with his hair mussed, how Ricky would sometimes switch to Spanish in the throes of passion and the way his voice had flowed around the liquidity of the syllables, Ricky making him drinks in his kitchen, Ricky gesturing dramatically with one hand, Ricky laughing, Ricky —

Liam gasped.

Ricky looked up at him. His eyes widened. "You. You stay away from me. Just stay away."

Liam halted. "O-okay." God knew, he had only done shitty things to this man, this younger man, this kid he'd had no business messing around with.

Ricky backed out of the room. He looked terrified.

Liam was confused and disoriented, but… did that make any sense?

THAT NIGHT, FINN was there, and he told him that he was making progress with Destiny, and that they were almost ready, that it would all be happening soon.

Destiny told Liam that he wasn't allowed to have any contact with Haysle, because she thought it would be a destabilizing influence for them both, but Finn assured Liam that he'd seen her and that she was fine.

So, Liam's schedule was altered to keep him away from Haysle. He was kept busy now, given duties outside the house in the yard. Destiny didn't like a tree trunk that was in the middle of the yard and she wanted the trunk dug up and all the roots removed and the hole filled back in, and Liam and a guy named Mick were out there trying to accomplish this with garden shovels.

The work was backbreaking but it was focusing somehow. He felt less hazy.

Of course there was less Destiny, so maybe that was why. Maybe she had been hypnotizing him and he hadn't been able to resist.

Liam brought the shovel back to the house three times with the intent of using it on Destiny, but he always stopped himself, remembering that if he killed Destiny, he'd have all her crazy drones descending on him.

To that end, he decided he would try to make friends with Mick.

They would take breaks from digging to have a bit of water and catch their breath, and during this, Liam would try to ask him questions.

"You, uh, you don't strike me as the typical MadCad fan," he said. "How'd you end up here?"

"Why don't I seem like a MadCad fan?" said Mick.

"I don't know," said Liam. "I mean, it's not a thing you'd expect straight men to —

"Who says I'm straight?" said Mick.

"Right," said Liam. "Trust Destiny to not give a fuck about people's sexual orientation."

Mick looked at him. "What are you talking about?"

"Finn says that Destiny makes all the guys have sex with her, so I thought..." Liam cocked his head. "Do you have hypnotism sessions with Destiny? They pretty hazy?"

Mick gave him a look, then, a sort of frightened-rabbit look, one that let Liam know that he was not entirely unaware of the fact he was being routinely sexually assaulted. But then he picked up a shovel and began attacking the tree roots with gusto. "Destiny says that in the spirit of love, there is no sexual orientation."

"Oh, she's curing you of being gay? With her pussy? That's fabulous." Liam shook his head and let out a sarcastic laugh.

Mick picked up the shovel and came for him, pointing the end of it at Liam's neck.

Liam backed up, arms up in surrender. "Hey, sorry, calm down."

"You don't know anything," said Mick. "You're some kind of interloper in the circle. I don't know why she wants you here. And every time Phineas shows up, everything gets worse. He's not good for her, and I try to tell her…" Mick sounded like he might cry. He went back to the tree trunk.

"You just told me you weren't straight," said Liam. "So, no matter how much she tries to convince you that there's no sexual orientation in the spirit of love, I guess it hasn't sunk in on a deep level." Then he wondered why he would keep prodding at this when Mick had nearly cut his head off with a shovel. He wasn't nearly as focused as he thought he was. He was actually coming untethered out here.

"What do you have against her?" said Mick. "All Destiny wants to do is help people."

"All Destiny wants to do is control people," Liam countered. "It's probably because no one loved her when she was a little girl and she's twisted and emotionally stunted. Sad story, really, but it's no excuse. She doesn't want to help you. She wants to use you."

Mick barked out a harsh laugh. "You don't understand anything." And now, he sounded defensive.

Right, well, Liam supposed he'd been a bit combative there, hadn't he?

So much for making friends.

Another day, he tried again, but he was more careful not to bring up sensitive subjects. "I, uh, make YouTube videos about *Hitgam?* You ever watch that show?"

"Yeah, I guess," said Mick. "But to be honest, I never was much into actually reading the original *Dusk*. I didn't honestly do a lot of reading."

"So, how were you part of the fandom?"

"I liked the artwork." He shrugged. "I watched the movies."

"The fan artwork," said Liam. "Like what Finn used to

make." Drawings of the characters, Maddox and Cade, typically in sexually suggestive positions, that was what Finn had made and sold at MadCad conventions. He'd even had a line of downright pornographic pieces that he'd sold sealed. No pictures of it appeared on the internet, and it could only be purchased in person, not through the mail. He'd sold those prints for exorbitant amounts.

Liam knew this not because he'd paid much attention to the MadCad fandom when Finn was selling things, but because he'd done research after the fact for a series of YouTube videos about Finn's connection to *Dusk*, a fanfic called *This Love*, and his murders.

"Yeah, that's how we met him," said Mick. "He was at a convention once, and I guess he and Destiny went to college together."

"Me too," said Liam. "We all went to college together."

"Really?" Mick leaned on his shovel, looking Liam over. "Well, that's interesting. That's why she wants you here."

"I don't know," said Liam. "I don't pretend to entirely understand her." Then he winced, because that was edging into combative again.

But Mick only laughed at this.

Liam smiled too.

The men shared a small moment.

Then they both went back to digging.

Liam glanced at the man, trying to think of something else to say, but wondering why he was even doing this.

Destiny had spent years indoctrinating this guy. If he was anything like the others in her group, Mick would kill himself at Destiny's command. What did Liam think he could do here? Have a few nice conversations with the guy and that would mean that Mick wouldn't stop Liam from killing Destiny?

He was fooling himself.

CHAPTER TEN

FINN WAS THERE more regularly, and sometimes Finn brought Liam food—extra food—and Liam didn't think anything of it, until he started feeling his heart start to speed up and his jaw start to clench and an odd feeling of bright goodness when he let out his breath.

It was early evening one night, and Finn had just dosed Liam with ecstasy.

It wasn't the first time it had happened.

Finn had dosed Liam before. The first time they'd kissed, Liam had been on the drug, and this was even after Finn knew that Liam'd had problems with it before, that he'd been hooked on it.

Liam hadn't taken ecstasy in over a decade. A guy his age, on a drug like this? It was ridiculous.

Finn found him and handed him off a pack of gum.

Liam stuck a piece in his mouth and chewed. "Is it tonight?"

"Yeah," said Finn. "I'm sorry about the E, but I thought it might be too much for you otherwise."

"Oh, great, Finn, thanks," said Liam. "I definitely want to be flooded with serotonin while I'm trying to murder someone. That's really going to make it easy to access my aggression. Perfect."

Finn furrowed his brow. "Shit. I didn't think of that."

Liam sighed.

"I told you I'm not always good at thinking things through," said Finn. "You want me to give you a back rub?"

Liam groaned, rolling his head on his shoulders. "Yeah, okay."

They were upstairs in the attic, which was Finn's bedroom, and they sprawled out on Finn's bed and Liam sat between Finn's spread legs, and the other man rubbed his neck, and Liam let the drug wash through him, and it felt good.

One thing about it?

He would have been nervous otherwise, but it was impossible to be nervous on ecstasy. That was good.

He wasn't sure about anything else, though, because ecstasy was a big love drug, which made him feel connected to everyone and happy and pleased and he was much more likely to sit near someone and touch their face and tell them how beautiful they were than he was to… to…

Finn seemed nervous. He bounced around the room, checking and rechecking his basket of lubrication and sex toys and then going to move a cell phone in the corner, which was propped up on a table near the sloped ceiling.

It took Liam a minute.

"You have a phone?"

"It doesn't have service," said Finn. "And there's wi-fi here, but I don't have the password. So, it's just a camera."

"You want to film this?"

"This is, like, huge, tiger." Finn stroked Liam's face, breathless. "It's a big deal, and when I have the videos, it helps. If I have them, I can keep it down for longer, you know?"

"Keep what down?"

"The need," said Finn.

"To kill, you mean?"

"Yeah, sometimes I can keep it under control by just watching the videos."

"Maybe watching the videos makes you want to do it more," said Liam.

Finn considered. "I don't know. I guess that's possible.

You said I couldn't be rehabilitated. But has anyone ever even tried?"

"To rehabilitate a serial killer?"

"I wasn't even a killer until Destiny made me one," said Finn. "I left them alive."

Liam remembered the girls Finn drugged and raped, the ones he'd seen in his dorm room on more than one occasion. He felt ill. What was going to happen after they killed Destiny and they got out of here?

"I can't go back to jail, Liam," said Finn.

Liam let out a laugh. It was hard to think like this. The ecstasy was making him feel all floaty and euphoric. "Yeah, okay, whatever, Finn. We'll figure it out."

"You mean that?" Finn looked up at him. "Really, tiger? Can I trust you?"

Liam turned to look at the phone. "That's your insurance. You film me doing this murder to Destiny, and then you take me down if I try anything." He laughed again. He rubbed his forehead, and then couldn't stop because it felt too good. "Sometimes, you're brilliant, Finn. Sometimes, you do think things through."

"Uh... I actually just did want it for... but that's a good reason to film it," said Finn, grinning.

Oh, shit, had Liam just *fed* that to him?

Finn came across the room and kissed him.

Liam groaned into Finn's mouth. Kissing on ecstasy was *good*.

Their tongues were slippery sweetness that consumed him. Finn's body was pleasure incarnate.

He swirled away into the effects of the drug and everything was chemically induced bliss.

When Finn broke away, he patted Liam on the cheek. "You wait here, okay?"

"Wait, you're leaving me alone?" said Liam. "I am on ecstasy here. I cannot be alone."

"I'll be back with Destiny, okay?" Finn gave him a grin and then another kiss. "I won't be gone long."

Liam groaned again. "Can we have music?"

"Yeah, I'll see what I can do," said Finn.

Then he was gone.

It seemed as though Finn was gone for several eternities, but when he was back, he had brought Destiny, and she was giggling and had her arms around Finn's neck.

Finn shoved her into Liam, who caught her.

Destiny looked up at him, and Liam could see her pupils were dilated. She giggled again. "Oh, he got you, too, I see."

"Yeah," said Liam, wrapping his arms around her waist. "Fucking Finn."

"Fucking Finn," said Destiny, laughing. She threw back her head. "Oh, I haven't rolled in, like, a decade."

"Me either," said Liam, laughing.

"Doesn't it make you feel like you're twenty-two again?" She dragged her hands over his chest. "It's like no time at all has passed. Like… I could do anything, like I could conquer the world." She closed her eyes and sighed. "Finn, you said there was going to be music."

"Yeah, working on it," said Finn.

Suddenly, the air was rent with the sound of Daft Punk's "Revolution 909."

Liam stretched his jaw, letting out a noise of utter jubilation. "Oh, perfect."

"Yes," said Destiny, eyes wide. "*So* perfect."

"I forgot how different kinds of music change everything," said Liam. He was rubbing his hands up and down Destiny's back.

"Me too." She dragged her fingers over his shoulders. "It's good."

"Yeah."

"We should dance!"

"We should fuck," said Finn, pressing himself into Destiny's back and pressing his lips into her neck.

"Oh…" said Destiny, letting out a throaty laugh. "So, *this* is your evil plan."

"Just wait," said Finn, licking a long line up her neck to her earlobe as she gasped. "Just wait until you see what I have planned."

Destiny yanked Liam's face down to hers.
He was kissing her.

CHAPTER ELEVEN

LIAM PANTED.

"CHOKE her." Finn's voice.

The music seemed to be inside Liam's head, and he could feel it throughout him, as if it started in his brain and pumped all through his limbs, all the way into his cock, which was lodged snugly in Destiny, and he was hard as fuck, but that was because Finn was lodged snugly in *him*, and he was always so fucking hard when his ass was full like this.

He remembered the first time they'd done this, how it had been pain and fear.

This was…

This was goddamned *heaven*.

"Come on, tiger," Finn's voice was labored, tickling his ear, so low that maybe Destiny couldn't even hear him.

"What are you whispering to him?" Destiny murmured. No, she couldn't hear. "No secrets, boys. Not from me."

"He says," wheezed Liam, "that I…" He brought up his hands to her neck. "Should kill you."

Destiny smirked. "Oh, are we replaying this, boys? Really?"

"Yes," whispered Liam, tightening his fingers around her neck.

Her eyes widened. "Ouch."

He tightened again, another notch, like a belt closing

around her neck. He felt as though he was concentrating very hard on something now, and the concentration felt *good*, the ecstasy made it all feel *so* good.

Her mouth moved. She couldn't make noise, though.

He was crushing her neck. He smiled at her. He started to move his hips in a different rhythm, getting deeper into her, and moving against Finn's cock, dragging that huge thickness in and out of himself.

He let out a noise, something unbridled.

Destiny was struggling.

It made her pussy move in interesting ways.

He fucked her harder. Last time she hadn't struggled, but last time, she'd been playing a game, playing both of them, and this time, *they* were playing *her*.

"Fuck, tiger," muttered Finn. "What the hell are you…?"

"Give me your goddamned cock," Liam said, gasping, squeezing, the ecstasy pulsing through him, his cock throbbing in time to the techno. "Give me *all* of your cock."

"Fuck," groaned Finn.

Destiny hit him.

He threw back his head and sighed.

She hit him again. It didn't hurt. She was getting weaker already.

"Like that, tiger?" Finn's voice was throaty.

"Just like that," Liam confirmed. "Just exactly like that."

Now, she was scrabbling at his hands on her neck, digging her fingernails into him, hard enough to make him bleed.

He didn't stop squeezing.

He just fucked her harder, and Finn settled into a perfect rhythm, moving just right against him, that perfect depth, that just-right good burning *stretch*, and now Destiny's movements were less, going fluttery and now her body was making odd spasms, which felt… kind of good? And now she was still.

Still.

He kept fucking her for a while after she stopped moving.

"Let go," said Finn, pulling his cock out.

Liam let out a noise of protest.

"See if she moves," said Finn.

Liam let go of her neck.

It was bruised. Red. Misshapen in an odd way.

Liam was still thrusting, almost absently, because the music was still riding him, still going through him like electric current, and he was a slave to the beat, to the drug.

Finn reached up, reached under the mattress, and he handed Liam a knife.

Liam stopped thrusting. "No."

Finn pressed the knife into Liam's hand. "We need to be sure."

Liam shook his head. "I already did this much. You do that part."

Finn gestured to the phone. "Come on, Liam. It's my insurance."

"No." Liam shook his head again. "What are you going to do if I say no?"

Finn licked his lips. "Remember how we had a conversation once about things I wanted to do with your dead body?"

Liam flinched—a whole body flinch—and the music somehow burst through him, and he felt as if a door had been opened, a dark, bad door, and now the drug had turned distorted and awful and he was afraid. He clutched the knife and pointed it at Finn. "Try it," he said in a low voice.

"Going to stab me, tiger?" Finn's breath caught in his throat. He sounded turned on.

I want you *to do it.* That's what Finn said in that beach house when Liam had told him the state of Virginia would be happy to kill him.

Liam swallowed, bringing up the knife. He traced the tip over Finn's collarbone.

"You don't want me dead, tiger. We were just... connected."

Liam swallowed again. "I do want you dead, Finn." He let out a long, slow breath. "I hate you."

One side of Finn's mouth pulled up. "No, you don't."

Suddenly, Destiny coughed. Her entire body came up off the bed in a convulsive explosion.

Liam whirled faster than he'd known he had the ability to do and plunged the knife into her throat.

Blood went everywhere.

III: RICARDO HERNANDEZ

CHAPTER TWELVE

RICKY HERNANDEZ HAD a boyfriend once who was verbally abusive.

He never hit him or anything.

And they didn't date for very long, but it had been long enough, Ricky supposed. He'd moved in with the guy, whose name was Phil. Phil Daxon. Ricky had met him when he was only a sophomore in college, and they'd moved in together quickly because it had been convenient due to when the semesters were starting and that kind of stuff.

But even if that situation hadn't happened, Ricky probably would have moved in with him anyway, because he had been really flattered by how into him Phil had seemed. No other guy had ever cared so much about Ricky, about every aspect of him, and at first, it had just seemed like a dream come true.

It took a while for Ricky to realize that a man who planned out his clothing and told him when to shower and refused to let him eat certain foods and freaked out if Ricky was two seconds late and didn't want Ricky to hang out with anyone except him was actually a raging controlling asswipe and not a loving and interested boyfriend with some fun kinks.

Ricky thought about Phil when he was locked up in the basement by Destiny, but then he thought about all kinds of stuff locked up down there.

There was nothing to do except think.

He got two bathroom breaks a day, only two, and these were facilitated by Tyler, who wouldn't speak to Ricky except to give him directions, and then Ricky got food, which was typically only cereal and sometimes he got milk and sometimes not.

Ricky thought a lot about the things that had led him to be attracted to a shit like Liam fucking Emerson.

If it hadn't been for Liam, he would not be here.

He'd gone out to investigate the location of that IP address because of Liam, and it had led him to be captured by Destiny Worth.

It had been stupid, and it hadn't made any kind of sense, and maybe Ricky should just blame himself for it.

Well, he was, he supposed.

It hadn't really been because of Liam, but because of Ricky's attraction to Liam, Ricky's wanting Liam to care about him.

That kind of desire, the desire to matter to someone, that was the same stupid shit that had gotten Ricky into that relationship with Phil.

But wasn't that what everyone wanted?

Wasn't that what love was all about?

The thing was, though, if Ricky was truly honest with himself, relationships never seemed to be about him mattering to other people, but instead about other people mattering to him. Every single relationship he'd ever been in, he'd poured himself into being a good boyfriend to the other guy, and the other guy—all the other guys—had taken him for granted.

And yet, Ricky just kept coming back for more. He had no self-respect, apparently.

He was attracted to exactly the wrong kind of man.

He even found himself feeling a little bit attracted to Tyler, who was obviously into Destiny and straight, and that was just like Ricky, really, to start having feelings for someone who was emotionally unavailable and also violent and possibly psychotic.

Well.

The violent psycho might be new.

Maybe he'd never fallen for a violent psycho before.

DESTINY'S STUDY WAS clean and soft and warm, and Ricky loved it there.

"You feel relaxed here?" she said.

"Yes," he said.

"Will you close your eyes and surround yourself with the most relaxing, safe place you can think of?"

"Okay," he said. He would do anything not to go back in that awful basement room again. Obediently, he closed his eyes.

"Where are you?" Destiny's voice seemed clearer now, louder, all-encompassing.

"Outside," he said dreamily. "Outside in a warm, sunny meadow with beautiful flowers."

"Very nice," said Destiny. "I want you to really feel as though you are in that meadow. See all the flowers, and feel the sun on your face. Listen to the breeze as it flutters leaves on trees. Smell all the smells of the outside world. Will you do that for me?"

"Yes," whispered Ricky.

"We'll stay here for a while. I want you to note this place, remember it, and return to it whenever you need to return to it. In a moment, we'll begin talking about some memories you have, but during all that, I want you to stay here in this relaxed place. No matter what you remember, you will feel the goodness and the sweetness of your safe place, all right?"

"All right."

"So, staying in that meadow, feeling the sun, hearing the birds chirping, I want you to think about your relationship with Liam Emerson."

RICKY SAT UP straight.

He was in his bed at home in his apartment.

Liam was there, also in bed with him, sitting up also, covers around his waist, his chest bare.

"What did you say?" said Ricky, feeling disoriented, as if something about this wasn't quite right.

"Are you ready?" said Liam.

"Ready for what?"

Liam reached out and took Ricky's hand. "It's the most amazing thing that I can think of, and I want to share it with you. He shared it with me, and now I want to share it with you."

"Who's he?"

"Phineas Slater, of course."

Ricky yanked his hand back. "What the fuck, Liam?"

"It'll bond us, Ricky," said Liam, grabbing his hand again. "You can't imagine how close we'll feel if we do it together. And we'll pick someone miserable, someone who won't be missed, someone for whom death will be a release from pain."

"You're crazy," said Ricky warily.

Liam sighed. "So, what you're saying is that you're not ready yet."

"I'm never going to be ready to do a murder pact with you. Is this a joke?"

Liam pressed into him, kissing him, running his fingers over Ricky's bare upper arm. "Remember what we talked about?" His lips moved over Ricky's jaw, tickling the small amount of growth there, since Ricky had just woken up and hadn't shaved. "Remember how we talked about how hot it would be if you got my permission before you talked to anyone?"

"Y-yeah," said Ricky.

Liam pushed him down into the bed. "So, just text me before you have any conversations today, okay? And if I find out you hid something from me, you know you'll get punished." He grinned, raising his eyebrows. "But I think you like your punishments, don't you, Ricky?" He was crooning. "You're my very bad boy, aren't you?"

And in spite of himself, Ricky was getting hard. He was confused and turned on and this… something about this…

"THAT THING YOU said to me?" Tyler was crouching down on the floor in the concrete room, setting a spoon down next to Ricky's bowl of cereal. "Actually, you might have said something to me about it a couple times, about whether or not I was *with* Destiny like that?"

Ricky was starving. He scrambled over to his bowl of cereal and began eating it, hovering over the bowl and shoveling it in, milk streaming down his chin, getting in his beard—because he had a beard now since he hadn't been allowed to shave in ages. "Um, sorry about that." His mouth was full and he didn't care about being polite and not talking while he chewed.

"Are *you* with her?"

Ricky looked up at Tyler. "Um, I'm gay." He set down his spoon. "I thought that was pretty obvious."

"Right," said Tyler. "Well, so am I. All of us met up through the MadCad fandom, and I've yet to meet a straight guy who was into *Dusk* at all, let alone into homosexual slash pairings of a YA paranormal romance novel."

"Right," said Ricky, nodding. "Right. Good point. Hey, I study fandom. I did a dissertation on—" He broke off. "Wait, so *are* you with Destiny?"

"I just noticed she started taking you into her study and doing those hypnotism sessions, and that's usually how it starts," said Tyler.

"How what starts?"

"Well, I don't know." Tyler stood up. "Sometimes I think I'm just losing my mind, because she won't acknowledge any of it happens, but I have memories of it. Weird, little pieces of memory that surface sometimes, but I just shove them down. But then you kept asking me that, you know. If

I was in love with her? If we were a couple. And it made the memories seem stronger, and I started to remember more."

"So, wait, what are you saying?"

"I guess, nothing like that happened to you? What do you remember about your sessions with her?"

"We talk about my past relationships," said Ricky. "I've suppressed a lot of really fucked up shit about Liam Emerson, and he, um, was kind of controlling and borderline abusive to me. I never experienced anything like that before."

"Oh?" said Tyler. "One time you were telling me about that Phil guy, though."

"Phil who?" said Ricky. "I didn't think you were ever listening to me when I babbled at you."

"I don't remember his last name. I think it was Phil. I do listen to you, and I remember that, because you said pretty much the same thing about him. You said he was controlling and borderline abusive and that you never experienced anything like that before."

"Um, I don't know what to tell you. I never had a boyfriend named Phil, and Liam is the only guy who's ever treated me that way."

"Huh." Tyler folded his arms over his chest. "And that's all she does with you?"

"Well, yeah. She says we're making good progress, and that I'll be able to get out of here soon."

Tyler nodded slowly. "Maybe I *am* losing my mind."

"You should talk to Destiny about it," said Ricky. "She can help you."

"She'll just say we should have more sessions," said Tyler softly.

"What do you think is happening in the sessions?"

"Never mind. I'm not really supposed to be talking to you." Tyler turned his back and walked out of the room.

RICKY PULLED A set of sheets out of his closet and handed

them to Tyler. It was strange to be back here, finally, away from Destiny, here in his old apartment. It was very strange. "Take these out to the couch. I'll bring the blankets." He turned back and took out a folded blanket. "I think you'll find the couch pretty comfy. I've slept out here a bunch of times when I just fall asleep watching TV."

"It doesn't have to be comfortable," said Tyler. "I'm here on a mission, same as you. I'll get it done, no matter what."

"Yeah, but isn't your mission making sure that I don't betray Destiny or something?" said Ricky with a smirk. "She doesn't trust me, and I can't even believe it. After everything she did for me, after she opened my eyes to what was really happening? Of course she can trust me."

"It's not about not trusting you," said Tyler. They were in Ricky's living room, and he set down the stack of sheets on the couch.

"So, then what's it about?"

"I don't know. She didn't share with me," said Tyler. He looked at him. "But I think she put us together for a reason. I think she could sense that we would work well together."

Ricky drew back, looking at Tyler. Was he imagining that, or...? He had found the man attractive, but back then, he'd thought Tyler was a violent psycho. He had thought that Tyler and Destiny had killed people, but now he knew that it wasn't like that at all.

Tyler seemed to regret having said this. He made a grab for the sheets. "Uh, I can probably make the couch up myself, if you want to—"

The sound of a phone ringing cut into the air.

Tyler got his cell out of his back pocket, looked at the screen, furrowed his brow, and then answered it. "The highest form of love," he said instead of hello.

Someone responded on the other end, probably with, "is sacrifice." Ricky knew all about the tenets of what Destiny believed, which was actually really noble and amazing. It had changed his life.

Tyler listened as someone was speaking on the other end of the phone. His hand tightened around it, his whole body going tense. "Wait, they're gone? When did they go?" A long pause. "What about Jennifer?" Another pause. "Fuck." Then a very, very long pause. "Absolutely. I'm on my way." He hung up the phone.

"What is it?" said Ricky in a quiet voice. He could tell from Tyler's manner that things had gone very, very wrong.

"I have to go," said Tyler. "You, um, don't do anything. Whatever the mission is that she gave you, just go on hold, okay?"

"Why? Who was that? Was that Destiny?"

"Destiny's dead," said Tyler.

Ricky took a step back. "B-but, she's beyond that kind of thing. I thought she'd attained a level of control over her physical form—"

"Naked and stabbed in the throat in Phineas's room, bled out on his mattress," said Tyler. "I never trusted that fuckwad." He put a fist to his mouth. His eyes were shining.

Ricky sat down heavily on the couch, right on top of the somewhat-spread-out sheets. "This can't be."

"I have to go," said Tyler.

Ricky stood up. "I want to go with you."

"No." Tyler shook his head. "No, you can't."

"But what do I do?"

"Nothing," said Tyler. "Do nothing. Just put everything on hold." He started across the room, heading towards the door to Ricky's apartment. Then he stopped. "I, uh, I could come back?"

"Yes, do that," said Ricky. "Please do that."

Tyler licked his lips. "Okay, well, then I will. I'll come back, Ricky." He turned again. He left.

Ricky sat back down on the couch.

He touched the sheet, feeling shell-shocked.

IV: THE OUTSIDE

CHAPTER THIRTEEN

FINN PULLED UP into the parking lot of Liam's apartment complex. He didn't park in a parking space, but just pulled up to the door to the building and turned back to look into the back seat. "Well, this is your stop, kids."

Haysle didn't know what to make of this. Finn was driving the car, and he was dropping them off, so where was he going after he left them here? They wouldn't be able to find him.

Liam pushed the door open and got out of the car. He beckoned for Haysle.

She got out too.

"Shut the door, tiger," said Finn.

"Hey, Finn, you can't just disappear," said Liam. "We may need to communicate about coordinating our stories with the authorities."

"I'm not getting caught again," said Finn. "Tell them whatever you want. They're never going to question me again, so I'll never contradict you. Shut the door."

Liam shook his head. "Shouldn't we have some way to—"

"*I'll* get in touch with *you*, okay, tiger?" Finn grinned.

Liam hesitated another minute longer and then he shut the door.

Finn took off, and the car turned around and pulled out of the parking lot.

Liam sighed and then they went inside the apartment

building.

They got to Liam's door and then realized it was locked. He'd had the keys when he was captured, but they hadn't gotten back their personal effects.

"There's an office." He pointed.

"Is anyone in there?" she said.

"I don't know. Even if there is, I don't know that what I want is witnesses that we appeared like this in the middle of the night." He touched the hoodie he was wearing. Some of the blood was seeping through, a dark stain that looked nearly brown. "I think I can get in a window."

It was lucky that he had a first floor apartment, Haysle supposed.

They went back outside and walked around the back of the apartment building, looking in windows until they were certain it was Liam's place.

Liam's window back here was indeed unlocked, and he took the screen out and pushed the window up and they climbed inside, tumbling down onto Liam's bed.

He shut the window, leaving the screen outside.

They both sat on the bed, next to each other, for several long moments.

"I need to get cleaned up," he said finally.

"Sure," she said.

"You probably do too."

They weren't hungry, because Finn had stopped at a fast food restaurant on the way there and gotten them all burgers and fries.

"Well, you go first," she said.

"We'll just... together," he said, getting up. He glanced at her. "Unless you don't... unless..."

"No, that's fine," she said. They'd showered together before, of course, and it hadn't always even been sexual, and there was no way that there was anything sexual about *this*.

But when they peeled off their clothing in Liam's small bathroom, he smelled like a mix of sex and blood, and her stomach lurched, and she had to struggle not to lose her fries.

They were quiet under the spray of the water, both doing a lot of scrubbing, all over, vigorous scrubbing.

Then, when he was turning to hand her some shampoo, she finally got a good look at his eyes, his dilated pupils, and she jerked back. "You're high." She hadn't noticed. How had she not noticed?

"Finn drugged me," said Liam, giving her the shampoo bottle.

She took it. "Some kind of hallucinogen?"

"Ecstasy," said Liam.

"Oh, of course," she said. She looked at the shampoo for a minute, and then she set it down and wrapped her arms tightly around his waist from behind, squeezing him for all she was worth, her breath catching painfully in her throat as tears surfaced. "Oh, Liam, Liam, I'm so sorry."

"It's wearing off," he said dully. "Anyway, it doesn't matter."

"It does matter," she said.

"You don't really want to know what I did tonight," he whispered. "I definitely don't want to know."

"He made it like he wanted it," she said. "Like he said at the beach house, when he wanted you two to kill her together. He made you have sex with her."

"I mean, there was sex," he said. "I don't know how forced I was." He wriggled out of her arms. "Sorry. I don't know why I—"

"MDMA is a *date rape* drug, Liam."

He turned and looked at her, blinking. "I mean... yeah. I guess."

"I *know*," she said.

His face crumpled. "But I've been on ecstasy before, and I can't say that the things I do on ecstasy are things I would never do any other time."

"Did he really give you a choice?" Haysle whispered.

"Well, no," said Liam. "I guess not. I thought I would have told him no if it was just me, but you were there. And Ricky was... And I thought maybe..." He turned away. "I guess it's good you weren't pregnant."

"Yeah," she said. "I guess it is." But this only made the tears start flowing harder out of her eyes. She sniffled and then picked the shampoo back up and began scrubbing her hair as hard as she could. "Destiny Worth was a monster. I'm glad she's dead. I'm glad you killed her."

"I stabbed her in the neck," said Liam.

"I'm glad." She was fierce.

He looked at her.

She shoved the shampoo bottle into his hands, moving under the shower head to rinse her hair. "I just wish we'd killed Finn too."

Liam turned the shampoo bottle over and then squirted some in his hands. "I don't know what we're going to do about him."

"What deal did you make with him?"

He rubbed shampoo into his head. "It was just about getting out of there. I didn't make him any promises about afterward. But, uh, I don't know about sending him back to jail. He seems a little too good at escaping."

"Well, he can't be free."

"You want to talk about…" His lower lip trembled. "You don't have to."

"It was stupid, that's the thing," she said, sniffling again. "Before it happened, I had all these thoughts about how I couldn't get away from him, because of that damned fence. But I didn't think that there was a reason he concealed my escape attempt from Destiny, and that I was valuable to him, and that if I tried to make it harder for him, he might have just decided it wasn't worth the effort. After it was over, I thought of twenty ways I could have stopped him."

"Hey." He shook his head. "Hey, it's not your fault."

She moved, letting him have the shower head to rinse his hair. "I didn't even try. I just laid down for him and let him do it. I laid there and thought about how it didn't hurt and how it wasn't so bad, and it mostly wasn't, except when he hit me."

Liam made a fist and drove it into the wall of the shower.

She let out a cry, jumping back.

He muttered a curse and examined the shower wall, which looked okay, and then looked at his knuckles, one of which was bleeding. He shoved it under the shower spray.

She cowered.

"Sorry," he said. "I asked you to talk about it. I shouldn't have... reacted..."

She didn't say anything. She was trembling. She hugged herself. "Um, I'm clean. I'll just get out. Is it cool if I put on some of your pajamas?"

"Of course," he said, turning to her. "Hey, did I... I didn't mean... Fuck."

She tried to smile. Mangled it. Fought with the shower curtain. Managed to get out and drip and shiver on the mat as she wrapped herself in a towel. "We shouldn't have— we should have gone straight to the station. The fact we came back here and showered and—"

He poked his head out of the shower. "Haysle, I couldn't go to the police covered in her blood."

"You were forced to do that. You were raped and coerced. Finn—"

"He filmed it. And I don't think I'm going to look coerced on the video."

She stiffened.

"Fuck," he said again. He closed the shower curtain.

"I'm..." She didn't finish her sentence. She huddled into the towel and left the bathroom. She dressed in a pair of Liam's sweats and a long-sleeved t-shirt. The sleeves were long enough that she could hide her hands inside them. She curled up on his bed, liking the feeling of being covered up everywhere. But she didn't get under the covers. She lay on top of them until he came in, wrapped in a towel, his hair dripping, rivulets of water running over his biceps.

She bit down on her bottom lip and watched him towel off and put on a pair of pajama pants.

He came over to the bed. "I can sleep on the floor if you want."

"Why would I want that?"

"I don't know."

She reached out and grabbed his hand and tugged on him until he came down onto the bed with her. Then she maneuvered them until they were laying on their sides, chests pressed into each other, faces inches apart.

"I know you," she said. "I know who you are. I have ever since I met you. I've had a sense of you."

"Haysle, that doesn't sound like something a detective would say."

"I'm intuitive as a detective," she said. "Sometimes, I just go with…" She drew in a breath. "With what I feel, even if I can't explain it. And with Destiny's murder the first time, I didn't turn you in, even though I felt like—"

"You didn't trust me then."

"No, no, I did," she said. "I trusted you, but I felt like I was being stupid. Even so, I went with what I felt. And I know you, Liam. And you're not whatever it is that Finn is trying to mold you into, okay?"

He licked his lips. "What if I am?"

"No."

He sighed, trying to pull away from her.

She held on tighter. "And, Liam, I need you right now."

His gaze found hers. "Haysle, if you try to depend on me, I will disappoint you. I am—"

"Liam." She let out a noise that was dangerously close to a sob. "What we just went through? I need you, because no one else will *ever* understand it."

He swallowed. "I guess that's true."

"She kept me in a room with nothing in it except a toilet and she didn't feed me and I had to drink—" Haysle let out a real sob, and then she swallowed the next one that started to come out.

"I'm so, so sorry." His voice was hoarse.

"I'm different now," she said. "I don't fit into the world in the way that I used to."

"I'm sure that after a little time has passed, and with some major therapy—"

"Liam, it's me and you. I need you. I am going to depend on you, and you're going to depend on me. And everything else… fuck everything else."

His eyes welled. "No, no." He cupped her cheek. His voice broke. "No, Haysle, sweet Haysle, I don't deserve that."

"I don't care. It's what I need from you. You will step up and give it to me." Now, there was steel in her tone. "You said you killed Destiny for me, partly for me, right? If it had just been about you, you wouldn't have?"

"Maybe I was just making excuses—"

"So, you do this for me now, because I need you."

He pressed his lips to her forehead.

"Promise me, Liam."

"I promise." His voice was a rasp.

She pressed closer to him. She wanted to be as close as she could possibly be. "Okay," she whispered. "Okay, if we have that, everything will be okay. I'm here for you, too."

He wrapped one thick arm around her, crushing her into his chest.

They fell asleep like that, touching everywhere.

CHAPTER FOURTEEN

RICKY FIDDLED WITH the empty styrofoam cup. It had contained coffee, and he was sitting in an interrogation room at the police station in Cape Christopher. "You had a case against him, didn't you? You nearly arrested him for the murders and not Phineas Slater."

"I'm just here to take your statement," said Officer Mitch Clark. "I'm not offering any arguments to what you're saying. You're the one who seems hesitant."

Ricky looked into the cup, and the tiny bit of brown liquid that clung to the bottom. Tyler told him not to do anything, to halt his mission entirely, and he'd tried, really he'd tried. But he felt *compelled* to do what he was meant to do, and even if Destiny was dead, that didn't mean that justice should not be served. So, he'd had to come here and do this. It was the right thing to do.

"Do you want some more coffee?" said Clark.

Ricky shook his head. "No, it'll only make me jittery and more nervous." He settled back in the chair. "It's sort of private, I guess. I feel embarrassed about it."

"Well, why don't we start at the beginning?"

"I guess you know that I had a relationship with Liam Emerson."

"Uh… no, I wasn't aware." Clark shrugged.

"Well, he sort of came onto me. He showed up at this bar where I usually go and he was really aggressive. Then it went from there. He…" Ricky was having a hard time saying this out loud. "He was… he's older than me, and he was a little bit, uh, there was a sort of dominance kink to… He used to order me around. Make me text him for permission to do things like, um, eat?"

"Right," said Clark. "Like that *Secretary* movie with James Spader."

"Uh… not familiar," said Ricky.

"Yeah, you were probably five when it came out," said Clark, shrugging. "Also, probably not really your thing, what with it being all about heterosexual sex…" He cleared his throat. "You know, I just watched it. I've never… it seems like a lot of work, ordering someone…" He cleared his throat. "So, you and Liam, with the kink. I assume this is important."

"Just that it started to become really… like, it overtook my life. He was making me ask for permission for everything, and I couldn't make my own decisions, and it wasn't hot anymore, it was just fucked up. And that was about the time where he started telling me things."

"Okay."

"Like confession things. About how he and Phineas Slater had killed those girls together."

Clark cocked his head to one side. "Uh, we have videos of Slater killing those girls. Alone."

"Well, who do you think was filming?"

Clark sat back in his chair, lips parting. "He confessed this to you?"

"He says there's more video, video of him, uh, molesting the corpses. He has it, though, Phineas never had those videos, so that's why it was never recovered as evidence. But Liam says it's always been the two of them, since college."

"And he just told you this."

"He wanted to do it with me." Ricky's lower lip trembled. "He would ask me if I was ready yet. He said it would bond us. He said…"

Clark blinked. "Well, it always seemed a little weird to me that he was living here, near Slater, all along, and they didn't even know about each other."

"Exactly," said Ricky. "Because they *did* know about each other. Anyway, when I started pushing back about it, telling him I was never going to kill someone with him, he, um, that's when he forced me to go out to that abandoned house, and that's how I was taken by Destiny Worth. He thought she'd hurt me, but it turned out that she had been fighting against the two of them all along. Did you know they left her for dead when she was seventeen? Tossed her body in the river. They thought they killed her, but she lived."

"Wait a second, what?" Clark shook his head. "You know, I'm not entirely familiar with this case. This was Dawson's case, and she's not here, so—"

"You can't trust Haysle Dawson. She's with Liam now. They're together. I don't know what he's convincing her to do."

"Well, Dawson and Emerson were taken, we assume by Destiny Worth—"

"They weren't taken. They just left. They went on some murder spree, and I think it ended at Destiny's house. I think they're the ones who killed her."

"Wait, what? Destiny Worth is at large. There's a warrant for her arrest. She definitely committed a murder in Cape Christopher—"

"Destiny never killed anyone," said Ricky. "She's a good person. She's helped me so much."

"Uh huh." Clark looked troubled. "You know what? You hang tight here for a bit. Let me get you some more coffee? Or, uh, a snack from the snack machine. Chips? Crackers?"

"I'm really fine," said Ricky.

"Okay, if you're sure." Clark got up. "I'll be back."

"I KNOW WE should have come in last night. Believe me, I know. But we were in no shape, and it was the middle of the night, and we would have had to get you out of bed anyway," said Haysle.

Liam watched her, feeling nervous, feeling out of sorts, not liking any of this.

They were in Captain Moore's office, and he had a coffee the size of a Big Gulp that he was holding with two hands as he stared at the both of them with wide, wide eyes.

"So, we're here first thing in the morning, and we can go through everything that happened. I'll start, and then Liam can — or... if you want to separate us, I mean — I don't know. Whatever you think, captain. We're still reeling, to be honest."

"Yeah, you both look like shit," said Moore. "Half-starved."

"She did that," said Haysle. "She did that to us, yeah."

"There was never enough food," Liam spoke up. "Just rice a lot of the time. Or cereal, sometimes without milk. Hungry all the time."

She turned to look at him. "Yeah. Me too."

"All right, first of all, we need to know where you were held," said Moore.

"Oh, yeah, I kept track of the route," said Haysle. "I, um, I emailed it to you."

"You did?" said Liam.

"I used your computer this morning," said Haysle. "I actually... I haven't been home yet. I need to get..." She touched her clothes. "These are Liam's." They were too big for her.

"Okay, let me look at that," said Moore, turning to his computer. He set down his giant coffee cup. "You know, we thought we had it cracked. I had this idea that, uh, that Quentin must have come from wherever it was that Destiny was, and if we tracked his phone's movements, we'd find her."

"Oh, you did think of that!" Haysle straightened, smiling. "But I guess it didn't work?"

"We found a place," said Moore. "It showed signs of being where Persephone, Worth's daughter, had been kept. And we found Robert Worth in a room in the basement."

"Alive?" said Haysle.

"Yeah," said Moore. "Stark, raving mad, though. And, um, practically starved to death, very weak. He went into a hospital, but he didn't recover. He died there, before we could really get anything from him."

Haysle swallowed. "Well, that sounds like Destiny."

There was a knock on the door. "Who is it?" called Moore, who was back at his computer screen. "Oh, here's your email."

"It's Clark," came a response.

"Come in," said Moore.

Clark entered, saw Liam and Haysle, and stopped short.

"Oh, Clark, look who showed up?" Moore grinned. "I'm in the middle of getting the story from them. What's up?"

"I'm with Hernandez," said Clark.

Ricky? Liam wondered if he should ask about him.

But Clark was still talking. "Uh, captain, I wonder if I could talk to you in private?"

Moore turned away from the computer and gave Clark an appraising look. "Detective, I'll meet you in the hall."

Clark nodded and then walked out.

Moore typed on his computer. "Okay, I'm going to have someone call the local PD in the locale where these directions are, but I'm going to go ahead and send out some uniforms anyway. If the local guys are not good with us being there, I'll just bring our guys back. Hopefully, they'll be willing to work with us. Let me just get this email off..." He clicked his mouse with a flourish. "All right." He got up from his desk. "Give me a second with Clark." He left the office and shut the door.

Haysle rubbed her neck and licked her lips.

Liam wanted to take her hand, but he didn't know if he should.

"Why wouldn't Clark talk in front of me?" Haysle chewed on her lip. "What's Ricky doing here? What did she do to Ricky? We have to talk about the hypnotism."

"Okay," said Liam. "I just... are you sure we need to be so completely honest about everything?"

"Yes," she said. "Come on, we can't conceal it, Liam."

It was true, of course. When Destiny's body was recovered, his DNA would be all over it. He hadn't come, so there wasn't semen, but he'd been sweating and he was sure he'd left his DNA all over her. It wasn't something he was going to be able to cover up.

Captain Moore opened the door abruptly. "Was Hernandez there with you?"

"Yes," said Haysle. "But we were all kept separate a lot of the time. I didn't see him until he was being carted off in a car and driven off. And here's the thing, captain, Destiny Worth had studied hypnotism, and I saw her put him into a trance, and I don't know what post-hypnotic suggestions she's put in his head, but—"

"Okay," said Moore. "This case just keeps getting weirder. But that, um..." He looked over his shoulder. "Hey, you hear that, Clark?"

Clark appeared in the doorway. "Are you two fucking?"

Liam looked away.

"Is that important?" said Haysle.

"Shit," said Moore. He blinked at Liam. "I thought you liked men." He looked at Haysle. "You're, um, not a man anymore, right? You wouldn't have let me get your pronouns wrong and not said anything, would you?"

"Liam is bisexual," said Haysle. "And I am a woman. And..." She let out a huge sigh.

"I'm not trying to be an ass," said Moore. "Seriously, I'm not. I was actually genuinely confused." He reddened. "Where's my coffee?" he mumbled, going back to his desk. He picked it up. "Clark, why's it matter?"

"Were you also fucking Hernandez?" said Clark.

Liam slid down in his chair. "I, uh, can be a little slutty."

Moore barked out a laugh. "Well, shit."

"I'm not saying Hernandez is not acting weird," said Clark. "Like I said, he was defending Destiny Worth. And I also don't know a lot about post-hypnotic suggestion. But he says that Emerson confessed to him that he and Phineas Slater have been killing together since college."

"*What?*" Liam shot up out of his chair.

Haysle's face went white.

Moore held up a hand. "Okay, Emerson, okay."

"We did like him for this." Clark pointed at Liam. "I mean, it was practically an airtight case until we found the Slater evidence. So, it's not out of the realm of possibility, captain, that's all I'm saying."

Haysle shook her head slowly. "You're going to try to arrest Liam for… for…"

"No one said anything about arrests," said Moore.

Haysle shook her head. "This is her plan. Destiny did this. She said this to me, yesterday. She was in her study, and she said it would be interesting to see if I would send Liam to jail or cover up his sins."

"What sins?" said Clark.

"No, no." Haysle shook her head. "There aren't any sins. She was just fucking with my head. She wanted to send us all out here and make us dance. Play a little game with us. But I trust Liam with my life. Liam saved me in that place. He did what he had to do in order to get us out of there, and he *protected* me. So, there's no way I would believe her horrible lies."

"Well," said Clark softly, "sounds like if he did have sins, you would be motivated to cover them up."

"No," said Haysle, glaring at him. "That is not what I'm saying."

"You know, let's just calm down," said Moore. "You two haven't told me anything yet."

"I think we're going to find a good lawyer first," said Haysle, getting up from her chair.

"Oh, seriously? Now, Dawson," said Moore. "Nothing makes you look guiltier than—"

"Seems to me you already suspect us," said Haysle, glaring back and forth at them. "Come on, Liam, let's get out of here."

"You can't just go," said Moore.

"Are we being detained?" said Haysle, raising her eyebrows.

"Fuck," said Moore. He pointed at Clark. "This is you,

you know that? You did this." He held up both of his hands. "Okay, look. Dawson, you go and talk to a lawyer, and we will set up a meeting. We will have a lawyer present, and we will do this right, so that everyone feels comfortable. But you should know, I can't just let this slide at this point. I have to open up an investigation into Emerson. Maybe into both of you."

Haysle only shook her head.

"I have to look into things," said Moore. "It's my job. And I'm sorry, but I have to place you on suspension. Can you turn in your badge and your gun?"

"I don't have a badge or gun, because they were taken from me when I was captured, tortured, starved, and raped," said Haysle. "So, no. This has been a great welcome, by the way. Thank you both. It's really good to be back."

She seized Liam by the arm and pulled him out of the room, down the hallway, and out of the station.

HAYSLE WAS SHAKING with rage as they got back into Liam's car. She didn't know what to do with the emotion, which seemed to be growing bigger and bigger by the second, and she was frightened it was going to explode. She wanted to break things.

She couldn't remember being angry like this, maybe ever. Certainly not in a long time. Maybe when she was younger, when she was a teenager and all her emotions were volatile. She felt as if the emotion was having her, not the other way around.

She was so angry that she didn't speak. She sat on her hands to keep herself from smashing her fists into Liam's dashboard. She clenched her teeth and focused on her breathing.

Liam drove. His car keys had been at home, since he hadn't driven his car out the day they'd been abducted. Her car, however, had been out at the scene. She bet it was in impound as evidence. She bet that after that little conversation with Moore, she wasn't going to get it back.

That thought made her feel even more angry.

But at some point, she realized that Liam was not driving back to his apartment, and she sat up straight, putting a hand down on the dashboard. "Where are we going?"

"I'm taking you home," said Liam. "You said you hadn't been there."

She licked her lips. Right.

Why did the thought of home wipe out all her rage in a wave of crippling fear?

She sat back in her seat, curling in on herself. "You'll come in with me?"

"Sure," said Liam.

"You won't leave me there alone?"

He glanced at her and then back to the road. "You doing okay?"

"No," she said with a bitter laugh. "No, of course I'm not."

"Yeah, that was a dumb question," he said.

Haysle's apartment was third row from the beach. It was typically rented out as a vacation home, by the week, at least in the summer, but she'd worked a deal with the landlord to get the winter rates all year long, which was still too expensive. It was a one-bedroom, and the one bedroom was an open loft that she had to climb up to with a ladder. She had a roof deck that she could see the ocean from.

She loved the apartment, but looking up at it now, it only produced dread within her.

Liam got out of the car.

She lingered inside, gazing up at the place.

She was thinking about the time that Finn had been inside her apartment, when he'd jumped down on her from the loft and tackled her on the ground, pressing his body into hers.

She shuddered.

She felt like vomiting.

Then she pushed open the door and got out of the car. She hugged herself, staring up the steps to the front door. The apartment was up on stilts in case of flooding. "Liam? I, um, can I stay with you for a while?"

He looked up at her. "That would be great, if you really wouldn't mind."

"I don't think I can be alone in this place," she said.

"Yeah, I don't want to be alone either," he said.

"So, I'll just grab some clothes and things, and my toothbrush, and…"

"Yeah, great," he said. He cocked his head to one side. "I mean, though, your place might be bigger than mine?"

She considered. Was it? "Yours has actual rooms. With doors."

"Yours has beach views." He shrugged. "I don't know, though. Is it the place or being alone? I know he was here once."

"I'd be okay here if you were here," she said. "But you need your computers and stuff. For work."

"Yeah, I'm definitely ready to hop right back into video editing," he said dryly.

She smiled at him. "Okay, well, if you're sure I'm not keeping you from anything by asking you to be here."

"I can do things on my laptop, anyway," he said.

"So, let's go get your clothes instead?"

"Yeah," he said. "Yeah, let's do that." He came over to her and wrapped an arm around her, kissing her temple.

She leaned into him, shutting her eyes, enjoying the solidness of him.

CHAPTER FIFTEEN

CAPTAIN JAMES MOORE rubbed his chin as he watched the footage of Ricky Hernandez's statement. They'd sent Hernandez out awhile ago, telling him to go home and get some rest and that they'd be in touch.

Moore wasn't sure what to make of all of it. He wasn't sure of anything except that he wanted more coffee, even though it was late in the afternoon and he knew that he shouldn't have any more, both because it would keep him up late and because it would settled sourly in his gut. His wife Monica would scold him about it when he came home. She'd ask, and he'd hem and haw, and then she'd tell him that she was only looking out for him and he'd feel awful, because of that conversation they'd had about retirement and how both of them were in agreement that they didn't want to be in such awful physical shape that they couldn't travel and have adventures in their twilight years.

"What do you think?" said Clark, raising his eyebrows.

"I think I want more coffee and I shouldn't have any," said Moore.

Clark laughed. "I could use a coffee with a dollop of something stronger in it, to be honest. When does this *end*, captain? This case keeps twisting in worse and worse ways. I'm beginning to feel like we're trapped in some kind of nightmare."

Moore let out a sigh. Clark wasn't wrong.

Clark scooted down in his chair, looking up at the ceiling lights. "Look, you know Dawson better than me. I worked with her on a few different murder scenes. She always seemed professional and no-nonsense to me, and I guess I did my best to mind my business, because I didn't want to be that guy about whatever her past is with the sex-change stuff."

Moore thought about correcting Clark and saying it probably wasn't a good look to say "sex change" but then he didn't, because the truth was that he didn't really know what was and wasn't a good look for all that. He didn't want to offend anyone, but he really couldn't keep up with all of it, even though he had tried. It seemed to him that these days, everyone was up in arms about something. "She's a good cop."

"Right, that's what I'd say," said Clark.

"And Hernandez, he's only worked with us in the capacity as an advisor, and his expertise is vampire fiction, so to say he might be susceptible to flights of fancy? Is that a leap?"

"Right," said Clark. "But what about Emerson? Because that guy has always just rubbed me the wrong way."

"Really?" Moore scratched the back of his head. "You got something in your gut about him?"

"Well, what about you? What's your gut say on him?"

"He's been real cooperative," said Moore. "He's given a lot of his personal time to helping us with the Slater case."

"Yeah, and is that somewhat suspicious that he's been so cooperative? Because maybe he's actually getting a thrill out of inserting himself into the investigation, which is a thing killers like that like to do."

Moore raised his eyebrows. "I don't know. Maybe."

"I just always felt like he was hiding something," said Clark. "And having sexual relationships with everyone from Slater to Dawson, it's... well, what kind of person does that?"

"Right, but they're all adults," said Moore. "It's none of our business. Besides, the fact that Dawson trusts him is a sign in his favor."

"Well, I don't know about you, captain, but I've made some terrible mistakes with people I've slept with. I'm attracted to women who aren't, um, sterling examples of moral uprightness?" Clark smirked a little. "And when I'm fucking them, I gotta say, I'm pretty blind to all that until it eventually shows up later. I'm not saying everyone is like me in this regard, captain, but I think it's common enough for people not to see the objects of their affection entirely clearly."

"Love is blind," said Moore, nodding. "But we have to tread carefully here, Clark. You heard that laundry list she spit out on her way out the door. Whatever happened to them out there, it sounds horrific. And with her being… with all angles of this case being what they are, we need to make sure we cross every 'T' and dot every 'I' because I'm not going to be accused of homophobia or transphobia or any other phobia or prejudice or hate or any sexual misconduct either. She said rape, Clark."

Clark slumped further in his seat.

"She's an officer of this department. This happened to her in the line of duty. We have a responsibility to her."

"But we have a responsibility to bring murderers to justice as well. And if Emerson is manipulating her, then we're doing her no favors by looking the other way."

"Good point," said Moore. He rubbed his temples. "Well, we can draft a warrant to look for these video files that he supposedly has and seize everything we can get. But I think we should get a statement from him first. If we're going for the warrant, I don't want anyone to be able to challenge that in a trial. I'd like some physical evidence, if I could get it."

There was a knock on the door.

"Yeah?" called Moore.

The door opened. "I know you said to hold calls, but we've heard from the officers out on the scene in Frederick County."

Moore sat up straight. "Yeah? Great. What do we got?"

"Destiny Worth's body. Naked. Stabbed in the throat.

Otherwise, the place is empty."

"I would have thought they'd all have shot themselves," muttered Moore.

"Maybe they did. Maybe we're going to find them all out in the woods or something."

Moore groaned. "Will they release the body to our lab?"

"Nada," said the officer at the door. "Apparently, there's a lab out near Ranson, West Virginia. It's, uh, the FBI satellite office where Delacroix and Reilly are based, and they want to send it there."

"Fine," said Moore. "That's actually perfect. They have state-of-the-art equipment and techniques, and I'm happy enough to have them handle it." He rubbed his hands together. "Well, if Emerson's DNA comes back on that body, that's going to be enough for me to get a search warrant, I think. What do you think, Clark?"

"Absolutely," said Clark.

RICKY DIDN'T FEEL good after his trip to the police station, and he wasn't sure why. He thought he would feel relieved, because he had done everything that he was supposed to do, and he had done as the mission required of him.

But there was some unsettled, niggling feeling that had taken up residence in the pit of his stomach, something that plagued him.

He knew he had another job to do, one that he wasn't supposed to do yet, not necessarily, but he began to ruminate on the idea of moving forward with it, because perhaps that was why he felt so unsettled. The problem was that he didn't know how to get in touch with Liam anymore.

He didn't have his old phone anymore, which had everyone's numbers programmed into it. He had been given another phone from Destiny, however, and she'd left recordings on it, relaxations she'd recorded for him to listen to. At first, listening to them had soothed him, but now, every time he heard her voice, he only felt more agitated.

But the point was that he had a phone.

Of course, Liam wouldn't have *his* phone. Even if Ricky'd had all the numbers of his contacts, it wouldn't have helped him.

He knew that Haysle's house had a landline, because it was a beach rental, and all of those houses were wired with home phone lines. He was pretty sure that the landlord paid for a phone line there. He didn't know that number, but he did know the address, and it wasn't hard to look it up online, because the information for all those rentals was posted on the website of the company that managed them.

So, he called Haysle.

But Liam answered. "Hey, Mom, I'm telling you, it's better if you don't bother coming down right now. Everything's crazy, and I swear I'll get in touch with you when we're ready to see you."

Ricky only breathed. So, Liam was at Haysle's. This hurt him.

Why did it hurt him?

He's an abusive bastard and a murderer. You cannot still want him.

"In the space between awake and asleep," he said into the phone, as he'd been instructed. "Remember everything." He hung up.

He let out a breath.

But he didn't feel any better.

Instead, he was wondering why he hadn't contacted his own parents. They must be worried about him, and he hadn't spared them one single thought since getting back. All he'd thought about was this mission that Destiny had given him, and it had seemed really important, but... but...

He thought about calling his mother, and then decided against that, and instead called a Lyft to just take him across town to his parents' house.

Surely, seeing his family would make him feel better.

And when he appeared in the doorway, his mother burst into tears, pulling him into her arms and saying she had known Saint Anthony would eventually bring him back to her.

His father was teary-eyed too, and Ricky found himself hugging them as hard as he could and crying too.

He stayed there for hours, and they tried to convince him to sleep there, in his old room. His mother said she wanted to be able to look in on him and know that he was all right.

But he said she could call him and he gave her the new phone number.

This began the questions about Destiny and about how he'd gotten a phone and his parents both vocally decrying anyone who would kidnap him and hold him prisoner, telling him there was no way that Destiny could possibly be a good person.

Ricky couldn't handle this.

It gave him a literal headache, as if his brain was trying to split in two.

He knew what he felt about Destiny was true, but he couldn't find any good reason for it. When he tried to defend himself, he sounded stupid. So, he simply got angry, yelled at them, and left the house, slamming all the doors on his way out.

When he got home, there was a car parked in his driveway and Tyler was sitting on the stoop in front of his townhouse.

Ricky had never been so happy to see someone in his life. Tyler would reassure him that Destiny was a good person. Tyler would help him make sense of *everything*.

LIAM MASTURBATED IN the shower and thought about Finn.

He wasn't sure why.

He told himself that it was disgusting to be wanting to masturbate at all, given everything that he'd just been through. His entire sex drive should be turned entirely off. He shouldn't want to have sex ever again.

But.

Well, someone had not sent that message to his erection.

He should ignore it. Erections happened for reasons that had nothing to do with sexual desire, after all. It was probably just some random physical response, his cock hardening for reasons unknown, and he should wait for it to subside.

Which.

It would.

It would be quicker to just take care of it, though.

And Finn's voice leaped to his brain. *Take it out and show it to me, tiger. Yeah, that's good. You want to stroke it for me? Nice, long, tight strokes. Tell me if it feels good.*

It was quick.

He felt ashamed of himself.

He scrubbed his body all over three times, as if he could wash Finn away.

When he got out of the shower, the phone was ringing. He'd called his mother, and she was being a mom about everything, wanting to come and see him, and he had forgotten that he'd told her to call back on that number, but it had to be her. No one else ever called Haysle's land line.

He picked up the phone. "Hey, Mom, I'm telling you, it's better if you don't bother coming down right now. Everything's crazy, and I swear I'll get in touch with you when we're ready to see you."

There was silence on the other end, someone breathing.

Not my mother. But this went through him like violence, and all the hair on his arms stood up straight. His breathing went erratic.

Finn?

"In the space between awake and asleep. Remember everything." The voice was male and somewhat familiar, but it wasn't Finn.

And it didn't matter, because he was suddenly awash in a memory, something long buried, something suppressed.

It was Finn. Finn and him and Cora Manning, and he had his hands wrapped around her neck. Cora was one of the girls whose body had been found in the freezer in Delaware.

She had been pregnant with Finn's child. There was a video somewhere of him and Finn having sex with Cora, but Finn claimed that he hadn't killed her, that he had no idea how she'd been killed.

Liam started, his whole body lurching.

He dropped the phone.

No.

That never happened. I never choked her.

He shivered, all the water from the shower making him feel clammy and frightened.

If it never happened, why did he remember it?

CHAPTER SIXTEEN

HAYSLE FIDDLED WITH her pen, looking down at the list of lawyers she'd made. She wasn't looking forward to calling any of them, because they were all defense lawyers, and she was usually on the other side of the courtroom, being interrogated by them during trials. Most of them intimidated her, but she figured that would be why they'd hire them.

Well, one of them, anyway.

She felt overwhelmed with the number of things that she needed to be doing, but getting a lawyer seemed top of the list. She was focusing on this now instead of getting food, for instance. She needed to set up a grocery delivery, but she was looking at lawyers. Liam had gone out to pick something up for them to eat.

She had told him she'd be fine on her own, but the fact was that being alone still felt terrifying. She supposed it was because of being in that room for so long. Then, after being set free, she hadn't really been alone much at all. Monique had stuck to her like a second skin.

And Monique was dead.

She'd watched that happen, Finn sticking a knife in the back of Monique's skull…

The door opened, and she stood up, her body on high alert, wishing she had a gun.

Her safe upstairs still had the extra ammunition she kept

in it, but no gun.

It was only Liam, coming in with a big paper bag. The smell of greasy food filtered into the apartment.

She stiffened. "You got fast food?"

He set it on the counter. "Sorry." He looked away. "I didn't think."

"It's fine," she said.

"I'm, uh, I'm a little…" He ran a hand through his hair. "Okay, first of all, I went by my apartment for some more of my stuff, and it's been ransacked. There's a notice that a search warrant was served on my property. They took my computer."

She drew in a breath. "Well, I guess we should have known that was coming."

"Have you heard anything from Moore?"

She shook her head. "No."

"Maybe it's too much to think he would have notified us as a courtesy?"

"I think he figured you'd be notified when they served the warrant."

Liam sighed. "Well, it's annoying, but there's nothing there. They aren't going to find video evidence of me and Finn…" He scratched his jaw. "Hey, uh, I gotta tell you something else."

She came over and began pulling things out of the fast food bag. She unwrapped a burger and took a bite. She chewed, waiting.

"I think Destiny planted memories in my mind with hypnosis."

Haysle chewed and swallowed, eyes wide. "Holy shit."

He let out a laugh.

She was thinking about it. "I guess that can happen. You hear about those people who try to uncover repressed memories through hypnosis and they get false memories because of the process, so I guess someone could do it on purpose."

"I would have resisted her, but… I was half-starved and they took my clothes, and —"

"It's okay. I know."

He picked up a carton of fries and popped one in his mouth. "So, um, there's more than one. They're all me and, uh, me and Finn killing together."

Haysle grimaced. "So… she somehow messed with Ricky, made him turn you in, and now you have false memories. You can tell they're false, though, right?"

"Uh… like, do they seem different than real memories?"

"They don't?"

"Not really?" He stuffed more fries into his mouth.

"Well, fuck, Liam."

"You don't think I really did do this stuff and repressed it somehow?"

"No." This was immediate and dismissive.

"I mean, obviously that's what she wanted. She wanted me to question my sanity, and to worry that I was really a murderer, and to lose my mind. Worse than I already have." He contemplated the fries ruefully.

"She said to me that there was more to the video of you and Finn and Cora," said Haysle.

"Yeah, well, funny, you know what memory is the strongest and the most vivid? Me choking Cora."

"But that doesn't even make sense," said Haysle. "Because when Cora was killed, she was already pregnant with Finn's child. She wasn't killed the night you guys had sex with her. She wouldn't have been far enough along."

"Right," said Liam, but he didn't sound sure.

"What?" said Haysle.

"Just, we're assuming that's the only time Finn fucked her is all."

Haysle grimaced. "No, you're right. Maybe that doesn't prove anything."

"How was she killed? What did the autopsy say?"

"I… I don't remember."

"Was she strangled?"

"Why don't I remember that?" She ate more of her burger. "That seems like an important thing to remember." She glared at the half-eaten bun and meat patty. "And now

I'm on suspension, so I don't know if I'm going to be able to find out. I wonder if they disabled all my logins to the various databases."

"I guess I could have choked her and then had to finish her off some other way, like Destiny."

"Right, you were covered in blood." She looked at him. "Do you want to talk about that?"

"Not really." He contemplated a fry. "Can I do it once with the lawyer, maybe?"

"Okay," she said, hunching up her shoulders.

"And the problem with the case, with Finn's killings, is that the bodies were buried and they can only approximate the time of death. So, even if I have an alibi for the night when one of those girls disappeared, that's not going to be enough to clear me. Furthermore, he kidnapped me and was holding me prisoner in a dog crate when he did some of those murders, which makes it hard for me to alibi out. He'd created a perfect, airtight case against me. I guess, this was the plan all along."

"Maybe this was Destiny's plan," said Haysle, thinking about it.

"Yeah, she wanted me out of the picture. She wanted Finn to herself. I would go to jail, and then maybe Finn would stop being obsessed with me."

"You think?"

"Yeah, I do. I think Destiny had a weird respect for Finn. She found him unpredictable and difficult to control, and that made him irresistible to her."

"But Finn's into you."

"Finn's just..." Liam bared his teeth. "Fuck Finn."

She nodded slowly. "Definitely." She eyed him. She was thinking that Liam was very even-keeled about this, that he was thinking through all the angles of it, and that he seemed... was this how a man would seem if he was innocent and was being framed for serial murder?

Oh, but she couldn't allow herself to stop trusting Liam. She had said to him that she had an instinct about him, that she trusted him even when it didn't make sense.

But…

I told you I'd be bad for you, Haysle.

Her stomach turned over.

He ran a hand through his hair again. "Having doubts?"

"No," she said too quickly.

"It's cool. Me too." He yanked out a stool at her breakfast bar and sat down at it. He looked through the rest of the fast food and found his own burger, only it wasn't a burger but a chicken sandwich. He took the bun off and fished out the tomato. He dropped it and it fell limply onto the wrapper.

She took another bite of her burger, thinking about how gross this food was and how she didn't care because she was hungry. *So* hungry.

"I mean… the thing is, I spent my whole life thinking I had killed Destiny on accident. So, I've believed for a really long time that there's some hidden darkness in me. I guess it's just not that far of a leap to think that…" He sighed. He took a bite of his sandwich and chewed. He swallowed. "And, then there's the fact that I had no problem killing her for real. I didn't even hesitate. That's really disturbing to me. I… I liked it."

"No, you didn't."

"I did." He nodded, sighing. "I was on ecstasy, though, so… like, I don't know if it means anything."

"Right. Chemically induced enjoyment," she said firmly. "It means *nothing*."

He ate more of his sandwich.

She stuffed the rest of her burger into her mouth.

They were quiet.

He set his sandwich down next to the discarded tomato. "The thing is, though, if I were able to repress memories, I would have repressed the memory of strangling Destiny. I thought I killed her, and I remembered that with startling detail, always. And I was wasted drunk at the time, so if I could have forgotten a thing, that would be a thing to forget."

"Right," she said, nodding. "Right."

"So, it doesn't make sense that I'd repress all this other

shit and leave that. No, I don't buy it. They are *not* real memories. I did not kill Cora. And I definitely didn't help Finn with his murders."

"You didn't," she said.

They eyed each other.

It was quiet again.

He was the one to finally break the gaze as he picked his sandwich back up.

She found her own fries and started to eat those.

They didn't say much more after that.

Later on, when they were entangled together in her bed in the loft, she felt his erection pressing against her before he recoiled, jerking back guiltily, whispering apologies in the darkness.

She brushed her fingers over his shoulder, pulling him close again. "It's okay, it's okay," she assured him.

"I don't... I don't want to..."

"I know," she breathed.

"Sometimes it happens, and I don't have any control—"

"I know. It's okay. It doesn't bother me." She tried to hold him closer still, tried to seal them into each other.

But he pulled away, rolling onto his back. He let out a series of noisy breaths. "When he... when you were... when he fucked you, did you like it at all?"

"*No.*" She jerked upright, gaping down at him.

"It's... I'm not asking because of some weird jealousy thing, and I'm not trying to judge you. It's okay if... I know he made you eat for him, and—"

"No, Liam, *God* no. He... Neither of us were even totally naked. He kept all his clothes on and he used lube, and I lay there and thought about how it felt like nothing and how glad I was that it didn't feel like anything at all. It wasn't even the least bit sexy. It was just... it was..."

"Okay," he said.

She lay down next to him, lying on her back. Now, they were not touching at all.

There was a long, long silence, no sound except the two of them breathing. It was so quiet she imagined she could hear the ocean, but she knew that couldn't be true, not from three streets away, not through the walls of her house.

"I'm so fucking sorry I asked you that," he said finally. "That was the worst thing I could possibly have asked you, and I—"

"You just asked because you liked it with him," she said. "But, again, Liam, you were on a serotonin enhancing drug. He drugged you on purpose to *make* you like it. It's not your fault."

"You don't have to do that."

"Do what?"

"You… you're always making me feel better about things, looking out for me, taking care of me. And I appreciate it, but not right now, not after I asked you that question, and you just had to relive—"

"It really wasn't that bad." She sighed. "I…"

"Do you want to talk about it? Because if you do, I want to listen, and I won't make it about me, I swear to Christ, I will not—"

"I guess I feel like it should have been the worst thing, but it just wasn't. Of all the awful things that happened to me there, it was the easiest. It was about as traumatic as having bad sex with my high school boyfriend. You know, Finn did it on me, and it was over."

"Okay," he said quietly.

"It's not like it was good, though."

"No, you just explained—"

"And I'm mad," she said. "So fucking mad. At him. But… but at *myself,* too."

"I get that," he said. "It's normal to blame yourself. It's normal to think you brought it on yourself somehow."

"I don't think that. I mean, *he* did it," she said. She sniffed. "I guess I could have fought him, though. I don't know why I didn't fight. It was like I knew what he was going to do, and I just… lay there and I—"

"That's really normal, too, you know that? To freeze?"

She sighed. "I guess you know all this stuff about being raped, since he…"

He sighed. "We're not making this about me, remember? Lots and lots of rape victims freeze. It's much more common than fighting. And it's probably smarter, anyway. Fighting increases the likelihood of getting hurt, and freezing is probably instinctual. So… I don't know if that helps, like, if it helps you feel less mad at yourself?"

"It does," she whispered.

They were quiet.

Minutes ticked by.

He drew in a breath, like he was going to say something.

And suddenly she started talking again. "I'm mad at myself for not being more traumatized, I think. It just… it wasn't that bad. You always think, like, if you get raped, it'll take something from you, like from your *soul* or something, but… but it was just *physical* and it didn't hurt and I'm fine, and when I have nightmares, they're about that room where she kept me, about that toilet, that jeering, dirty toilet—" She broke off in a sob.

"Haysle?"

"Yeah." Her voice was tight.

"Can I hold you?"

She felt some taut, horrid thing in her release. "Please," she breathed, rolling into his warmth.

He tightened his strong arms around her.

She burrowed into him, and she started to cry.

His body was shaking too.

They held onto each other, sobbing—mostly silently—for a while. A long while.

But then she was tired, and the sobs seemed to leave her, if only because she was too exhausted for the emotion, not because she'd come close to exhausting the well of awfulness she felt about it all. She wasn't sure that would ever happen.

But that was enough of that for now.

She lay her cheek against his chest, resting on top of his warmth. "We'll just do this for a while, I think. We'll think of horrible things and we'll cry. And we'll just have to keep telling ourselves the same things."

"What things?" He stroked her hair softly.

"That it's not our fault," she said. "That there's no set way to react to trauma and that our reactions are valid. That we'll get through it."

"I don't know, Haysle. That all sounds a little too healthy for someone as fucked up as me."

She let out a chortling snort.

He laughed too. He stroked her hair.

"But you'll try it anyway," she said.

"Yeah," he breathed. "Yeah, I will."

CHAPTER SEVENTEEN

LIAM WOKE UP with a start to see Finn there, at the foot of the bed, tickling his bare foot.

Liam turned to look at Haysle, next to him, sleeping soundly, and then back at Finn. His heart rose into his throat.

Was this a dream?

Finn gave him an easy smile and backed up, crooking a finger, beckoning Liam to come with him.

Liam got out of bed carefully, slowly, trying to gauge the way the air felt. Did the air feel as though he was dreaming or did it feel like reality? He couldn't tell. In dreams, things always felt real.

The ladder creaked realistically as Finn was descending it and as Liam went after him. On the bottom floor, there was a light on in the living room, a lamp covered in a sheet to dim the light, because Haysle didn't want to sleep in the pitch dark, and she didn't have any night lights, though she had said they needed to make a grocery list.

Finn went into the kitchen area and sorted through the wrappers from the fast food, grinning. He found some cold french fries and started eating them.

Liam sighed. What was this?

Finn beckoned again.

Liam came closer.

"You want to go on a ride with me, tiger?"

"No," said Liam.

Finn reached out and cupped Liam's face. "Am I going to have to kill her?"

Liam slapped his hand off. "You leave Haysle alone."

"What if I asked you to run away with me?" said Finn.

"And go where? And do what?" *Why didn't I just say no?*

"I don't know." Finn sighed. "Just be together, maybe?"

Liam rolled his eyes. "I'm calling the police." He started for the landline.

Finn stopped him, propelling him backwards into the refrigerator. He pinned him there with his forearm, holding it tight against Liam's throat, and he scrabbled behind him for a knife from the knife block on the countertop.

Liam struggled.

Finn put the flat of the knife against Liam's cheekbone. "Not going back to jail, tiger."

Liam's breath came out in harsh huffs.

"You said we'd work something out."

"I was rolling my face off," said Liam.

Finn shook his head. "I know you felt it, tiger. When I was inside you, you felt it."

Liam swallowed.

"We're... when we're together, it's powerful. You want me."

"Maybe," said Liam. "But that's not enough."

Finn let go of him. He pointed the tip of the knife at him. "Turn around."

"Why? What are you—"

"Turn around, so that I can tie you up," said Finn. "I can't have you calling the police the minute I leave. I need a head start to get out of here."

"You shouldn't have come here." Liam turned around.

"I told you about how I don't think things through." Finn pressed into him from behind, taking his wrists, kissing his neck. He pulled Liam's hand behind him and crossed them, and Liam felt a zip-tie sink into his skin.

Liam grimaced. "Ouch, zip-ties, seriously?"

Finn kissed his neck again. "Sorry, tiger." He reached

around and rubbed his hand over Liam's crotch.

Liam's stupid cock was hard immediately—fucking erection machine lately, seriously. He grunted.

"Well, hello," said Finn, delving into the flap of Liam's pajama pants.

A dark current went through Liam, pleasant and awful. "Don't." His voice wasn't strong.

Finn took him out.

Liam felt the cool air on his skin. His cock pulsed.

But Finn just left him that way, hands bound behind his back, hard cock sticking straight out of his pants, and Finn fled without even saying goodbye.

CHAPTER EIGHTEEN

"YOU DID WHAT?" Tyler was pacing in Ricky's apartment, pacing in front of the couch where the bedding was still sitting out, because Ricky hadn't put it away, not if Tyler was coming back.

"I had to," said Ricky. "It's the mission. I don't have a choice not to. It's like I hear her voice, and…"

Tyler stopped pacing. "Yeah, okay, I get that. But she's dead. And, uh, she wasn't supposed to be killable. So… we're all a little confused."

"Is she really dead?" Ricky laced his fingers together. Destiny had told him that she had ascended to a plane of existence in which she could heal herself from any injury, and one of the others, a woman named Jennifer, had told him that she'd witnessed Destiny's cuts healing up before her very eyes.

"She's really dead. I saw her body. I touched it. It was cold, and her neck was…" Tyler gestured at his own neck. "Blood, so much blood."

Ricky looked down at his laced fingers, unable to know how to process all of this. He was thinking about his parents, how they would react if he told them that someone could heal wounds with her mind. They would tell him it was crazy, and he remembered that there was a time when he would have thought it was crazy as well.

But then…

The long stretch of time in that room in the basement, with only Tyler to come to see him, twice a day, bringing food.

When he'd first been locked up, he remembered having a thought about Stockholm syndrome, and now he'd welcomed Tyler into his home. His parents would think that was crazy too.

But thinking anything else about Destiny felt *wrong*. It made his head throb painfully.

Ricky unlaced his fingers and spread his hands. He looked up at Tyler. In a very small voice, he said, "Did you ever see her heal?"

Tyler's lips parted. He didn't say anything.

Ricky put his head down.

Tyler sat down on the couch next to him. "I don't know what I saw."

Ricky turned to look at him.

"I feel like I can't trust half of the things I remember over the past few years," said Tyler. "I feel like, when I first started traveling with Destiny, that things were really great, and that lately, everything has just been kind of awful."

"Awful?" Ricky couldn't believe this. "What are you saying?"

"I don't know," said Tyler. "They didn't want me to leave. They said I should go and get you and bring you back, and when I said I wasn't going to do that, that's when they kicked me out, and I don't know where they went."

"We're cut off from the rest of the group?" Ricky's voice was going shrill. "Why did you do that? Why didn't you let me come with you?"

"Look, you're not part of the group."

"What?" Ricky was wounded. "Yes, I am."

"No, you're a mark," said Tyler. "She wanted to hurt you. Or maybe hurt Liam Emerson, and you were a tool to accomplish that, but she didn't care about you. Of course, I don't think she actually cared about any of us."

Ricky drew back.

Tyler vaulted off the couch again. "Shit, I can't believe I

just said that out loud. I think it, but saying it…"

"I *am* part of the group," said Ricky. "Why else would I be defending her to everyone out there even when they look at me like I'm crazy?"

Tyler started to pace again. "When I first joined up with her, it wasn't even really my thing. I went to that MadCad convention with my boyfriend Keith. We were both MadCad fans, but I thought the thing with Destiny was a little out there, and I'm not the least bit artistically inclined, so when he wanted to start taking the classes, I was just along for the ride. There was one class, and then another class, and then another, and they just kept getting progressively more expensive. And then she was saying that we should just come work for her and we'd exchange labor for more training, and it was all Keith could talk about, so we sold off half our stuff—man, we had this gorgeous apartment, really nice stuff." He looked around Ricky's place, wistful. "You've got great taste, you know? I used to, as well."

"Thanks," said Ricky. "I guess… Keith, he, um, left the group?"

"He shot himself in the head," said Tyler.

In spite of himself, Ricky gasped. He remembered that Destiny made people do that, of course he did, but he had just compartmentalized it somehow, or changed the narrative in his head so that it wasn't really death but just noble sacrifice, and now, that wrong feeling was increasing.

"It was, uh, not that long ago, at the house in West Virginia, the one when there was the big raid and Haysle Dawson was there. I was with Destiny at the time, me and Monique were. Everyone else shot themselves when the police showed up. We went and met up with others after that, the ones who were still alive."

"I'm… I'm sorry for your loss," whispered Ricky.

Tyler stopped pacing. "Keith and I hadn't touched each other in years. Destiny said that our energy would be depleted if we gave in to sexual activity, and Keith really bought into it." A long pause. "I mean, I did, too." He ran a hand through his hair. "I think that's when these doubts started, though, when he died? At first, I was just numb about it, and I was even more devoted to her, because everything else was pain, and doing whatever she said was a distraction from all that. But then, I started to realize that I hadn't had any chance to grieve, because Destiny didn't want to act like he even mattered, even though she said that the sacrifice was the greatest honor anyone could ever achieve. She barely ever wanted to mention his name again, and Keith was my everything." Tyler clenched his hands together, and his lower lip trembled for a minute. "So, then, slowly, I just..." He came over and sat down next to Ricky. "I don't think she could heal herself, no. I think she lied to us all."

"But... but..." Ricky lifted both of his hands. "What about the mission?"

"I don't know."

"I went to the police and told them about Liam."

Tyler nodded. "Yeah, it really sucks you brought the police into this."

"I can't undo it."

"Can't you? Just tell them you changed your mind and you don't want to talk to them anymore, that you've decided you'd rather just move on."

"But Liam is a murderer and an abusive bastard."

"Is he? Or did Destiny just convince you of that during one of her sessions?"

"What are you talking about?"

Tyler looked around. "You have a computer?"

"Um, of course. My laptop is over there." Ricky pointed.

Tyler got up and went over to pick it up. "You on Facebook?"

"Do I look like a boomer?"

Tyler let out a little laugh. "Right. How old are you?"

"I'm twenty-five," said Ricky disdainfully.

"So, Instagram?" Tyler opened the laptop and began typing. "You got an Insta?"

"Sure," said Ricky. "What does this matter?"

Tyler navigated to Instagram and clicked over to Ricky's

personal pictures. He began scrolling back, back, back in time.

"What are you looking for?"

Tyler squinted, ignoring him, continuing to scroll. Eventually, he stopped and handed the laptop to Ricky. "Oh, look at that. Phil."

Ricky looked at the picture. It was from when he was in college, and it was him and Phil Daxon. He blinked at it, and it was as if his brain was struggling to make sense of… of…

"You told me you never had a boyfriend named Phil," said Tyler. "But look. There's a picture of the two of you together, looking very cozy."

Ricky snatched the laptop from Tyler and reached out and ran his fingers over the screen. "But I…"

"She gets in your head," said Tyler in a soft voice. "I know about that."

"What does this mean?" Ricky was trying to reconcile two sets of memories, one with Phil's voice, one with Liam's. They were fighting each other, both seeming equally real. In fact, if he were to pick one, he'd be more confident the memories of Liam were real. They seemed *so* real. He set the laptop down and got up from the couch. He left the living room and went into the kitchen. There were dishes in the sink, and he began to rinse them and load them into his dishwasher, needing to *do* something to drive away the discomfort of his thoughts.

"Hey," said Tyler, leaning against the doorway. "You all right?"

Ricky slammed a dish down into the dishwasher. "She changed my memories of Phil to Liam? How?"

"Hypnosis is good at making people believe things," said Tyler. "I think that's what she did to us. Even if she didn't do those sessions, she did other things, broke us down, made us certain of things that didn't make any sense."

"Well, I only have memories of Liam confessing murder to me," said Ricky. "I don't have memories of Phil doing that."

"She mixed totally false memories in with the real ones,"

said Tyler.

"No," said Ricky. "You don't know that."

Tyler didn't say anything.

Ricky turned off the faucet. He shook water off his fingers. "Why did you come back to me? Why didn't you stay with the group?"

"I think I'm having, like, a crisis," said Tyler. "I think all my belief in her is fading out. I think I wanted…"

"So, you came to me?"

"You said I could come back here."

"Yeah, but…" Ricky dried his hands on a hand towel. He looked at Tyler. "Are you, like, attracted to me?"

Tyler shifted on his feet. "Are you not attracted back?"

"No, I am, but… I don't know if… you kept me locked in that room, you know? So, I'm not sure if any attraction to you isn't supremely fucked up."

"Right," said Tyler, bowing his head.

It was quiet.

Tyler cleared his throat. "I'm not trying to… I only want to sleep on the couch. And if you don't want me here, I can go."

"Why didn't you want to bring me to them?"

"Well, I'm afraid they're going to decide to, uh, to sacrifice themselves. They were talking about it, but I spoke out against it."

"Why did they listen to you if they told you to leave and not come back?"

"This was before that," he said. "I told them that if Destiny had been killed, and we were always sacrificing for her, that we'd be sacrificing for nothing, and that it would be pointless. They agreed we should find out more information first. Someone said that maybe Phineas Slater had figured out a way to steal Destiny's power, and that he'd absorbed it when he killed her, and that maybe if we all did the sacrifice, our essences would go into Phineas, which no one wanted, because we all hated him."

Ricky thought that seemed really complicated.

"I don't want to die," said Tyler. "Do you want to die,

Ricky?"

Ricky slowly shook his head. "No."

"Anyway, I'm going to get out of here," said Tyler. "I'm sorry that I came here at all."

"No," said Ricky. "No, it's okay. You can stay. You don't have anywhere else to go. But, um, but I have to go back and talk to the police. I can't just give up on the mission."

"Even if the mission is all false?"

"I *can't*," said Ricky fiercely.

LIAM CLUTCHED HIS phone to his ear, wincing at his ex-wife Belinda's shrill voice coming through the receiver.

"…and even though I heard you were free and back here, you weren't in your apartment, and you don't have the same phone number, and how was I supposed to get in touch with you?"

"Well, the phone number… I could have kept it, I guess, but I wanted something fresh, just wipe it clean." Why was he trying to explain this to her?

"You could have given me your new number," she said.

"That's what I'm doing now," he said. "And as for my apartment, there was a search warrant, and I have a lot of things I'm dealing with, Belinda."

"I hear that man who took Madison, that awful Slater person, he's out there again?"

"He's not going to bother you," said Liam. He didn't think Finn would go back after Madison again, anyway. "Madison is actually the reason I called. You and I are divorced, Belinda, and I don't need to get in touch with you. You don't need to get in touch with me. It was *your* idea to get divorced, you remember that?"

She sighed heavily. "Seriously?"

"And I'm… involved with someone now."

"I know about that Ricky boy," said Belinda. "You told me that Madison met—"

"No, someone else."

"Oh." She chuckled darkly.

"Look, Madison and me… I was helping her with her blog. She and I were spending time together regularly, and…" He found his voice losing strength. Fuck, he was such a coward. He should have called Madison herself with this.

"You want to start that up again?"

"The opposite, actually. I don't know if you know what happened to me at all, but, uh, I'm… I don't know if I'm up for it with her, but I didn't want her to think that it was about her. I was hoping you could tell her I was, uh, ill."

"Ill?"

"Like, mentally."

"Liam? What did happen to you?"

"If I—*when* I feel better, I'll get in touch with her. You know, if she wants. I just… right now I…"

"You're always such a prince, Liam," said Belinda in a low, sarcastic voice. "I can't imagine *why* I wanted to divorce you."

He grimaced. "Yeah, I'm not saying I don't deserve that, Belinda, but bad things happened. I lost track of… of everything when I was being held captive there. They starved me. They left me chained naked to the ceiling and they… they…" He didn't want to say any more of it out loud.

"Jesus," breathed Belinda.

Then it was just quiet.

"Liam," she said finally. "I'm sorry. I'm so sorry. I—"

"Can you just apologize to Madison for me?" His voice broke.

"Are you okay?"

"I need to hang up."

"Of course, I'll talk to her, but if you need anything—"

He *did* hang up. He stuffed his phone into his pocket and wished he hadn't called her in the first place.

"NO, I'M GLAD you came in," said Regina Biggs, who worked at the facility where Persephone Worth was housed. "I think she'll want to see you, if you think you can wait a bit? She doesn't like her schedule being disturbed, but I know she was fond of you, and a familiar face will be good for her."

Haysle wasn't entirely sure why she'd come here. There were a number of other things that she should be doing besides visiting Destiny Worth's autistic daughter, things that would help her get her life under control. And yet, here she was anyway.

She had never had any real confirmation from Destiny that Persephone had been born of incestuous rape by her father, but then that didn't seem like something Destiny would want to talk about. It didn't excuse any of Destiny's behavior, not in the least, but it did make Haysle wonder if that was why Destiny searched so long and so hard for adoration and love. She had never found it from her father, Haysle supposed, and so now she needed to have a massive group of people to control, all of them ready and willing to literally lay down their lives for Destiny.

And yet, through all of that, she'd been drawn to Finn, who was just as erratic and cruel and incapable of love as Destiny's father.

It was tragic in so many ways, for Destiny herself, but especially for all of her victims.

"I didn't know if she'd still be here," said Haysle to Regina. "I was afraid that she couldn't stay."

"Well, we're very resourceful here when we need to be," said Regina. "I have personally sought out grant money and private scholarships and anything I could do to find funds for our residents here, but in Persephone's case, it turned out that once her uncle's will was read, he'd left everything to her, so it's all in a trust, and it's earmarked for her care, and she can stay here as long as she likes."

Haysle looked around at the place. It was pleasant enough, she thought, but sort of institutional, and a bit like a hospital. She wasn't sure if she'd like it here herself. "And does she? Want to stay? If someone… if a person wanted to care for her in their home, would…?" Wait, what was she offering?

"Oh, well, in a case like Persephone's, honestly, a place like this is often the best fit," said Regina. "You have to realize that Persephone suffers from crippling anxiety, and one of the best ways for her to cope with that is a very rigid schedule, and that is often best provided in an institutional setting. She loves that every day, she does the exact same things. Furthermore, she needs a lot of attention and care, and one caregiver in a home often can't meet the demands and needs of someone like Persephone, not on their own. It would be better, even in a home setting, for Persephone to have someone coming in to assist with everything."

Haysle nodded slowly. "Sure, I suppose I can see that."

"Persephone has been making amazing progress since she arrived," said Regina. "I feel that the setting she was in before was very distressing for her and aspects of it may have even been abusive, I don't know. But her anxiety levels have actually come down a good bit just from having a positive and predictable environment. Everyone here loves her. She's one of our favorites."

"So, she does like it here?" said Haysle, and for some reason, her eyes stung.

"I think so," said Regina. "And we like having her. You know, working in a place like this, not all of the residents are easy, but occasionally, you get a connection with someone like Persephone, who's just, well, delightful in her own way. She's very smart, and she loves flowers. We have a garden she's been working with, and she's been researching flowers on the internet, and she can talk a blue streak about it, and she will, of course. When you see her, expect to be given a full run-down on the care and growing of various flowers."

Haysle smiled. "All right."

"If you wanted to come and visit again, somewhat regularly?"

"I would," said Haysle. "If that's okay, I think I would."

"That would be wonderful," said Regina.

Haysle sat and waited until Persephone was free and had a point in time in her schedule when she could see Haysle, and then she was shown to Persephone's room, which was covered in pictures of flowers, beautifully done.

Persephone bounced up and down at the sight of her, a huge smile on her face. "I remember you. You're Haysie, and you're the one who brought me to my new home here."

"I am Haysie," said Haysle, her heart swelling at the sight of Persephone, who looked so much better than she had before. Her cheeks seemed a little fuller, her hair a bit more lustrous, and she was grinning widely. "And I'm sorry I haven't been here to see you in a while, but I'd like to come more often, if that would be okay."

"That would be okay!" Persephone was jubilant. "Do you want to see my flowers? Do you know about Phalaenopsis orchids? They grow on other plants in the wild, but in your house they can grow anywhere. They can take water out of the air. They don't even need dirt."

"I didn't know any of that," said Haysle. "Did you draw these pictures?"

"I drew the pictures," confirmed Persephone. "This one is an orchid." She pointed. "So is that one. But that one was when I was learning to draw them, and it's not as good."

The pictures were very well done. Haysle was impressed with the girl's talent. "I think they're beautiful."

"Yeah," said Persephone. "That's what people say, but they're wrong. This one isn't as good." She was flatly matter-of-fact about this.

Haysle couldn't help but smile at the girl's manner.

They chatted a little longer about flowers but then Persephone retreated suddenly, pointing at a clock in her room. "Time for afternoon walk now. You have to go. You can't stay anymore."

"Oh," said Haysle. "I see. Well—"

"Have to go." Persephone hugged herself, biting down on her lip, looking nervous. "It's time for you to go."

Haysle saw what Regina was talking about, the extreme anxiety about her schedule. Haysle held up both hands.

"Don't worry. I'll go now. Everything will be fine, Persephone. Just fine."

After Haysle had left and was driving away, she thought about the way the world worked, how teenage girls like Destiny got pregnant with unwanted children who they didn't deserve to have, especially when Persephone was so clearly still traumatized by whatever had happened to her, still so full of anxiety about small things, and how other people who were ready for children and responsible, didn't get pregnant.

She thought about men like Destiny's father, who abused his daughter, about how he hadn't deserved his child either.

It was disgusting, and it made her angry.

So much ugliness in the world. So much pain and so many people hurting and hurting each other. Maybe once upon a time, she'd thought that by being a police officer, she could make a difference, make the world better.

Maybe she did, sometimes, at that.

But there was a deep well of awful out there, a flood of it.

CHAPTER NINETEEN

FELIX ROWAN LEANED back in his chair and eyed Liam. The lawyer smoothed out his tie, eyes wide. "So, wait, you're saying that Slater came to you and said that he would hurt Haysle if you didn't do this thing with him?"

Felix was the lawyer they'd decided to go with for this case. He wasn't cheap, but then Liam could afford it, what with the money his YouTube videos were making from ads. And Felix was one of the few defense lawyers who wasn't the least bit intimidated by the Cape Christopher Police Department. He could work a deal with the prosecuting attorneys, play nice when he needed to, and he'd built up those relationships for that purpose. But he also had no problem metaphorically taking off the gloves and bloodying his knuckles, putting those very relationships in jeopardy if need be. He was fearless.

Liam shook his head. "No, it wasn't quite that blatant. But I knew that Haysle was being kept prisoner in a room in the basement by Destiny, and the only way I could stop her was to cooperate with Finn. Finn could have easily done this another way. He had freedom I didn't have. But my only way of getting us out of there—all of us, including Ricky Hernandez—was to play along with him."

"Right, right, right, okay," said Felix, sitting back up and picking up his stylus. He scribbled some notes on his tablet.

"Anyway, then the night that we did it, he dosed me

without my knowledge with ecstasy."

"Oh, shit," said Felix. "But I guess you can't prove that? Like, you didn't go straight to the police and get a drug test to prove you were under the influence?"

Haysle spoke up from next to him. "Well, if Moore hadn't been hostile towards us, maybe that could have happened."

"Wait," said Felix, picking up his tablet, fingers flying over it. He cocked his head and scrolled through search results, and then he grinned. "All right, it's not like weed, which stays in your urine forever, but there is a hair follicle test that can detect whether its been in your system in the last ninety days, so *boom*." He scribbled something else on his tablet. "I'll get that test set up for you, Liam. I assume you're willing to do that."

"Absolutely," said Liam, taking a breath, feeling a little bit of triumph trickle in. There would be evidence of that, at least, which would help.

Felix looked up at him. "Great. As you were saying?"

"Uh, Finn went and got her. We, um, we danced together to music. She had been dosed too."

"That'll be detectable in her autopsy." Felix scribbled again. "Keep going." He motioned with the hand not writing.

Liam blew out a breath. He didn't want to talk about this. Just thinking about it was starting to make him aroused again, and he hated that. "Uh, we got undressed. There was, um, some foreplay and preparation, which I submitted to, so I don't know... I mean, I did not want to engage in sexual intercourse, but I didn't fight it. So, if we have to try to prove—"

"You let me worry about our strategies," said Felix. "All I want right now is what happened. You're saying preparation?" He raised his eyebrows. "Can you clarify?"

"Oh," said Liam, shrugging. "I just mean, lubing and stretching because it was like... I was the... middle."

Felix blushed. He cleared his throat. "Well. If I had any idea what you..." He looked away. "What did I think you meant?" he muttered. "So, that started happening, then," he said briskly, making that motion with his hand again to keep going.

Liam glanced at Haysle. He hated doing this in front of her. Talking about it. Thinking about it. "Uh, and then, Finn told me to choke her, and I did. I did that until she, um, stopped moving."

"And then you stopped."

"Well…" Liam drew in a breath. "The ecstasy made everything feel—"

"Okay, well, how long after she was dead did you—"

"She wasn't dead," said Liam. "She-she coughed. There was a knife—"

"Wait, where did this knife come from?"

"It was under his mattress," said Liam. "Okay, so, let me go back. So, um, she wasn't moving, and we were both, like, still… thrusting, and he pulled the knife out, tried to make me take it from him and said that we had to be sure, and I said no, I said that he should do it, because I had already done the, uh, the other part. But we were disagreeing over that, and then she coughed, and I just… it was like I didn't think, I just did it." He made a stabbing motion with his hand.

Felix's eyes were wide again. He didn't say anything.

Haysle's shoulders were hunched in. She wasn't looking at him.

Liam sighed heavily, his own shoulders slumping. "I'm going to jail, aren't I?"

"No," said Felix quickly. "No way."

Haysle looked up at him, hopeful. "You sure?"

"Oh, come on, you're a homicide detective. You going to charge a kidnapping victim with murder?"

"I…" She spread her hands. "Honestly, I never worked homicide until this case. I always worked in robbery, and this all seems so complicated."

"No, there's no case charging you with Destiny Worth's murder," said Felix. "Besides which, you have this added element of Slater in the mix, and he's public enemy number one, so, I don't think it would fly. Adding in the fact of all the people who have killed themselves on Worth's orders? They wouldn't charge you, because she's clearly dangerous, and lethal force used against her is justified, especially because you were being starved and raped and chained up naked from the ceiling… That's a non-starter."

"Even though we tricked her?" said Liam. "Even though we lured her up there?"

"Slater did that," said Felix. "Not you."

"What about the fact we didn't try to run?" said Haysle. "Both of us had chances—"

"You couldn't climb that fence," said Felix. "They had guns. You were physically and psychologically weakened. You were held captive. End of story. There's not a case to be made that you should have just run for help or something."

"But you hear stories, like about women who kill their abusers, and—"

"Well, if there's a reasonable idea that a person could just go to the garage and take the car and go to the police, you know, instead of stabbing her sleeping husband, that's a different thing than this. There was no reasonable way for you to get out of there. And Liam, it doesn't seem as though you had a choice. Slater, you have a previous relationship with him, in which he held you captive?"

"Yeah," said Liam.

"And so, you're already afraid of him. He's already demonstrated to you how dangerous he is?"

"Yeah," said Liam. "But he's never hurt *me*."

"But you thought he would hurt Haysle if provoked? In fact, he *had* hurt her, right, because we just went through her statement about his raping her."

Liam nodded. "So, what you're saying is that this isn't my fault."

"I'm saying that they're not going after you for this. It's a minefield for them, and they wouldn't risk it, no way. But I did manage to get access to the search warrant they drafted to get into your place, and…" He scrolled through his tablet. "So, the reasoning here is that your DNA was found on Worth's body, and that this contributed to a narrative from a witness that you and Slater murdered and raped women together. They were looking for evidence of that in your apartment. If you get charged with something, it's going to be that. They're looking to tie you to Slater's murders."

"Yeah, okay, I guess we knew that," said Haysle, sighing.

"But this is good," said Felix, "because I think we alibi you out of those murders."

"I don't know. The timing is pretty vague," said Liam.

"Nope, we have video," said Felix.

"Oh," said Liam, blinking. "I guess, when they were first questioning me about this, they hadn't found the video yet."

"The videos are all time stamped, and there is the time of the actual murder, right there. So, I've requested that evidence, and our strategy, I think, is going to be going through that and finding out where you were, and anything that we can use to prove that you were *not* with Phineas Slater, which we're going to find, and this is all going to go away. I don't even think you'll get charged, because when we go in to sit down with them, we will bury them with our evidence and they will back off."

"And if they do charge him?" said Haysle.

"Well, then we're going for the hypnotism stuff, and we're calling in experts and all that," said Felix. "But that's going to be quite the expense, so let's table that unless we need to go there."

"And you don't think they'll charge him for Destiny?" said Haysle. "Because I guess there is DNA evidence."

"There's DNA all over that woman, most of it they can't identify," said Felix. "I'm guessing when the other members of the cult found her, they just put their hands all over her. So, lots and lots of different DNA signatures. But they've also got Slater on there, his DNA. And there's no murder weapon."

"Finn took it with him," said Liam quietly.

"But he killed two other people on our way out of there," said Haysle. "What about those murders? Is that something they could try to pin on Liam? They'll probably be able to see that they've been done with the same knife, and there may even be traces of Destiny's blood in their wounds, because the knife was bloody."

"Okay," muttered Felix. "Uh, that's, you know, not Cape Christopher jurisdiction."

"Well, neither is Destiny," said Liam.

"Right, that's a good point," said Felix. "It *is* the state of Virginia, and I can represent you there, if such a thing should materialize, but we may want to bring in someone local additionally, someone who would have relationships with the prosecutors in Frederick County. My feeling is, that's kind of a sleepy little community there, and they've already given the bodies to the feds, and they're going to be happy enough to just push all that off their plates, if they can. We're going to have to play that by ear. It's easier for everyone if all of this is charged to Slater, however. And, as sad as it is, I think that making things easier is a lot of times pretty motivating for police departments, who are overworked and underpaid civil servants." He gave Haysle a little wink.

She rolled her eyes. "Yeah, I'm sure that's your typical opinion of the police."

"Come on, you can't be a good defense attorney without a good relationship with the police," he said, grinning at her.

She sighed.

"Bottom line, you guys, is to stop worrying about this and try to work on recovering from this crazy, traumatic thing you went through."

Liam looked at Haysle, and she gave him a weary smile.

Recovery. Was it even possible?

Haysle spoke up. "Okay, well, there's one more thing, and that's that Destiny specifically said to me that Cora Manning was the work of Liam and Finn together, and Liam has a planted memory of that."

"That's way out of Cape Christopher's jurisdiction," said Felix.

"Right," said Haysle. "Right. But we did recover her body, and we did examine that evidence, those girls in the freezer. I don't know that Finn was ever formally charged with that murder. We had nothing to link him to it. I had that in the pool of things I was going to charge to Destiny, I suppose."

"Trust me, you both need to relax," said Felix. "Go home, have a cocktail, get under the blankets."

Haysle nodded again, but it was hesitant. "Right," she said once more, in a low voice.

RICKY SHOOK HIS head. "No, it wasn't like that. He didn't give me names or times or anything like that. I didn't want to know details."

Clark was leaning across the table in the interrogation room. "Well, if there are specifics that you can recall, it's going to be really helpful."

"Are you saying you didn't find the videos?" said Ricky, feeling worried, feeling confused, feeling his head start to throb again, with the warring thoughts and memories inside.

"Definitely nothing like that," said Clark. "But there was one video, and it had actually been recently downloaded to his computer, but it's old, and it's him and Slater and a girl, and it's a... well, they're... but there's no violence, just basically amateur porn." He cringed. "Sorry. I could have put that better."

"Was it one of the girls who died?"

"It was a girl whose body was found in a freezer in Delaware," said Clark.

"Oh, right, the Cora Manning video," said Ricky. "They didn't turn that over as evidence, did they? That video originated because Destiny Worth sent it to Haysle Dawson. If you look into her work email account, you're going to find it. But she just sat on it, don't you think that's suspicious?"

"It is," said Clark. "It definitely is." He began to ask Ricky more questions about the video.

Ricky told him everything that he could remember about it, and as he did, his headache began to fade, and he wondered if the headache was a sign that he was running into memories that had been altered.

"Okay," said Clark. "Well, I think this is all we need from you for now, but we may need to call you back in for more."

"Are you going to... arrest him?" Ricky wasn't sure what he wanted to hear.

"The truth is that we don't have a lot of evidence," said Clark. "So, we're still looking. This is a pretty sensitive situation due to some various elements, but I feel strongly that if Emerson is a danger to Dawson, and if he's as abusive as you're saying he is, then, well, I'm not going to let it go, I'll just tell you that."

Ricky bit down on his bottom lip. "I should, uh, maybe tell you something about that abusive stuff?"

"What?" said Clark.

Ricky swallowed. "Okay, well, when I was captured by Destiny Worth—"

"Wait, I thought you said that Destiny didn't really capture you? Are you changing your mind on that?"

"I..." Ricky twisted his hands together. "Okay, I don't really know what happened, so I'll just tell you this. I was in a room, all alone, just a concrete room, and I got two trips to the bathroom a day and some cereal. And, uh, while I was in that room, I would think about things, all kinds of things, and one of the things I thought about was this boyfriend that I had named Phil Daxon, and he was... he was abusive in all the ways that I remember Liam being. I just... remembered him again last night when I saw a picture of him, though. Before, I had forgotten all about him, and I thought that... that Liam..."

"I'm really confused right now," said Clark.

"Destiny Worth made me go to these sessions. She'd have me close my eyes and relax, and she sort of... I would kind of go into a trance."

"Shit," said Clark. "This hypnotism stuff is real, then." He tossed his pen. "So, everything you're saying about Liam Emerson is just planted?"

"I don't know," whispered Ricky. "I just don't know

what's real anymore. If it's true, you'll find evidence, right?"

"If you're not sure of this, why are you here right now?"

"It's the mission," said Ricky. "It's the mission, because Destiny wants me to do it, and I have to do it. It's... it's justice."

Clark groaned. He dragged a hand over his face. "Gotta say, Hernandez, this is all starting to fall apart here."

Ricky hung his head. "I'm sorry," he breathed.

WHEN RICKY GOT home, Tyler was in the kitchen, chopping fresh fennel bulbs and pomegranates.

"Where'd you get groceries?" said Ricky.

"Uh, I took cash from Destiny's desk while I was there," said Tyler. "I thought I could do something to say thanks for letting me crash. This is just the salad. There's some chicken marinating in the fridge. Is it okay?"

"It's great," said Ricky.

"How'd it go with the cops?"

"I don't think they believe me," said Ricky.

"Can you stop, then?"

Ricky leaned against the refrigerator. "How did *you* stop? Doing what she was telling you to do, I mean? How did you break out of it?"

"Like I said, I think it started after Keith died. It was slow. But you... the stuff you said to me about Destiny and me being a couple, that... that helped me."

"Oh, yeah, you said that to me before, back when we were in that room." Ricky shivered, thinking about that room. "I still don't understand what you thought she did in those sessions."

"I remember bits and pieces of it sometimes," said Tyler. "Not all of it, which is kind of a mercy, so I don't know if I want to."

"But what do you remember?"

"Just things. Like this vibrator she had, it kind of curved around so that there was a little bit of it that tucked into her, uh, her pussy—I see her putting it in, and the other part is on her clit, and then she—" He squared his shoulders and went back to the cutting board, sorting through the slices of the fennel. "Then I blank it out, but I think she was raping me."

Ricky flattened himself into the refrigerator. "What?" he said softly. "Why would she do that?"

Tyler shrugged, using the knife to scoot the fennel slices away and then beginning to chop the fronds. "I don't know."

"You're not attracted to women," said Ricky.

"I'm well aware," said Tyler.

"But she said that sexual desires were a sacrifice," said Ricky. "That we had to jettison it and give it up to receive the blessings of—"

"Yeah, I know all the things she said."

"That doesn't make *sense*." Ricky glared at him.

Tyler looked up from the cutting board. "What's that in your voice?"

"Just… if I have false memories, then maybe you—"

"She wanted me to forget this. She did it while I was hypnotized. She tried to put in suggestions to make me repress it, and I guess it came back because her programming was breaking down."

"But *why* would she do that to you?" Ricky was starting to shake. "Especially if she needed a vibrator to even, like, get off. Why bother with you at all?"

Tyler set the knife down and turned around, leaning back into the counter. He folded his arms over his chest and eyed Ricky. "I don't know. But she had a group of people that would follow her around from place to place, doing whatever she said, even killing themselves for her, and I think maybe she liked that. And maybe the idea of getting a gay man to fuck her, maybe that… maybe that really got her going."

"*Gross.*"

"I think she was simply a gross person."

"But…" Ricky clenched his hands into fists and then

released them. "But… when I think of her, I *feel*…"

"I think she wanted you to feel that way."

"Why?"

Another shrug from Tyler. "I don't know, not exactly. There was a house in, uh, another part of Virginia, a big house, the one where she kept her daughter."

"Daughter?" Ricky didn't know about this. "She has a daughter?"

Tyler nodded. "Yeah. And she was always trying to get up the nerve to sacrifice her daughter and then not being able to do it, like that was a sticking point for her."

"She tried to kill her daughter."

Tyler blinked. "Now that you mention it, that's very fucked up, isn't it?" He went back to the cutting board, as if he couldn't talk about this while looking at Ricky. "It's like, she convinced me to think a certain way, and I still do about a lot of stuff, but now, I'm realizing that's a fucked up way to think about your own kid."

"I remember when I thought she was awful," said Ricky. "I remember, before I was captured, when I thought… Is that how I *should* feel about her?"

Tyler began to transfer pomegranates and fennel to a large wooden bowl. "I was making a point, and we're getting away from it."

"Okay, sorry." Ricky let out a disbelieving laugh, not sure if he quite cared if the conversation remained linear. He was spiraling off into deep insanity here and he didn't even know which way was up.

"At that house, in the basement, there was a man that she called the father. Always like that, with 'the' in front of it. She kept him in a room like yours, in the basement, and she fed him, but she didn't do much else. He was pretty pitiful, and this seemed to please her. Although there was this one time, when we were leaving that house, and she said something to me about how it was weird, because as much as she thought it would be satisfying to tear him down, some part of her just wished she could make him love her."

Ricky thought about this. "So, you think he was a bad

father? Because, like, we've all heard that abuse warps people." He squinted. "No, that's not it, actually, it's like a combination, like, you have to be born with a certain psychological bent, and if your parents love you, you're usually harmless, but if you're abused and you have that brain thing also, you usually turn into a violent psycho."

"Huh," said Tyler. He was still tossing the salad, even though it looked plenty tossed to Ricky. "I don't know what kind of father he was, but I think that Destiny, for whatever reason, needed more love than a regular person needs. I think she needed single-minded devotion from as many people as possible, and that no matter how much she had, it was never enough. That's what I think. I don't know if it was that pitiful half-starved man in the basement's fault or not. I kind of can't think of anything that would excuse all the shit Destiny did."

"So I shouldn't think she's… this wonderful being."

Tyler stopped tossing the salad and leveled his gaze at him. "You should not."

Ricky's lower lip trembled. "B-but what if I *do?*"

"We'll just talk each other out of it," said Tyler quietly. "I mean… or you find someone to help. I won't impose on you if—"

"I'm not kicking you out of my house," said Ricky. "I feel like no one else understands me right now." He drew in a breath and then he took three steps across the kitchen to stand right next to Tyler. He put a hand on the other man's upper arm.

Tyler flinched.

Ricky pulled his hand back.

"No, I didn't mean…" Tyler's breath came out noisily.

"You said that you were attracted—"

"But I haven't been touched by another person like that in years, and it feels wrong somehow."

"Okay," said Ricky.

"I mean, I guess except Destiny." Tyler's face twisted.

"I don't think that should count."

"Good," said Tyler. "I don't either."

They just looked at each other.

"Maybe we just work up to it?" said Ricky.

"You sure you don't want to kick me out?"

"Positive."

Tyler gave him a small, almost shy smile, an expression Ricky hadn't seen on the other man's face before. "Uh, the salad has a dressing, but I'll do that later, to keep the fronds from getting soggy."

"Okay," said Ricky, smiling back at him. "Do you want help with the chicken?"

"Not much to do except preheat the oven."

"Well, I can do that," said Ricky, his smile widening. "I'm very good at setting the temperature on my oven, actually."

CHAPTER TWENTY

DAYS PASSED, AND Haysle tried to relax, but she couldn't.

Liam and Felix were spending a lot of time together, going over every date they could, assembling alibis for each and every one of Finn's murders.

This left her alone in the house, which would have been fine, even without a gun, but then Liam told her that Finn had come to the house one night, had been up in the loft with them, and she was livid that he would have kept it from her.

Liam said maybe it was a dream, but they both knew it wasn't a dream.

And there was something about the way he wouldn't meet her gaze that let her know that the problem was deeper than Finn breaking into their house, that Liam had some odd sympathy for Finn.

She thought of the time that Liam had gone to meet Finn in Delaware, when she'd found him in that bunker, tied to a chair. He'd been under Finn's influence then, willing to do whatever Finn asked him. After Finn was locked up in prison, Liam had gained ground, pulled away from Finn. But whatever had happened between the two men while they were held captive in that house with Destiny, it had bonded them. There was some tight tie between them now, something stronger than whatever had held them together before.

It should have appalled her.

But she only felt a sort of numb resignation to it.

This was part of Liam, his affection for a serial killer, and she was in love with Liam, so it was a thing she accepted.

Once, she would have packed up all his clothes and things and put them out next to the door and informed him when he came in the door that she couldn't have him in her life until he excised Phineas Slater from his.

But that wasn't an option now.

Things had happened to her in that house too, and she was altered. She could not be alone, that was certain. The only person she did want to be with was Liam. Something had been put into her in that house, she had discovered, something small and growing, and it changed her. It changed everything.

So, the first order of business was to get out of this apartment and go somewhere else. She broached the idea with Liam in a businesslike manner, that they should just officially move in together, and that they needed more space than either of their apartments afforded them.

She had already picked out several options, places inside gated communities that came with installed alarm systems. She was planning on adding several deadbolts to all of the outside doors.

"I'm a little preoccupied with the case right now," Liam said. "I won't be able to help move."

"That doesn't matter," she said. "I have nothing else to focus on. It'll be good for me. Let me take care of it."

So, he did.

And she took care of it, though admittedly, she used a lot of Liam's money to do that. He hadn't talked a lot about how much more popular his YouTube videos had gotten after he'd started that series on Finn and *Dusk* and the murders, but he was making bank from ad revenue and he had Patreon subscribers sending him money every month as well, and he didn't seem to mind if she spent what was necessary.

Once, she would have kept tallies, a spreadsheet with all

the expenses, dividing them entirely in half, a running bill for herself to pay him back. Partly because of her own pride and partly because she would not have wanted to feel beholden to him.

But she didn't feel that way with him. It wasn't like that with them at all. Things between them were deeper than that, and there was no owing each other. They were connected, end of story. And pride?

Well, that had been leached out of her when she'd stuck her face into that grinning, smug toilet to take her first drink of water.

It was amazing how quickly a person could move two apartments if she was really focused on the task and she had money to pay for help.

She was disappointed at how fast it was, and how soon they were settled into their new place, because now she had nothing to focus on.

Now, she began to notice that Liam took long showers several times a day.

Now, she began to think about one final piece of the puzzle, one thing that was going to bother her if she didn't know the truth about it.

Now, she called Catherine Wilson, the person who'd been roommates with one of Destiny's victims and who'd first told Haysle about Lola Gem, as Destiny had called herself, and her group of new age college girls who'd had bonfires and made Destiny's first sacrifices.

Haysle didn't tell Catherine that she was not officially a police officer anymore, and Catherine didn't ask. Instead, Haysle asked again about the other members of this group. Catherine said she didn't remember anyone else by name. Haysle pressed her to look through old photographs and scrapbooks, to go hunting for anything from her college days. She begged her, telling her it was very, very important.

And the next day, Catherine got back in touch with Haysle with an old college newspaper. She sent a picture of a photograph, printed in smudged black and white, of an Earth Day celebration. A group of girls all lounged, half posing, on a bridge on campus that went over a small stream. They were young and brash and smiling, wearing crowns of daisies on their heads, Destiny in the midst of them in a crop top. The caption read, *Flower girls in spring enjoy the Earth Day festivities, L to R Trina Manning, Cora Manning, Harlow Walker, Destiny Worth, Monique Wilder, and Libby Knox.*

Haysle's finger brushed at her phone's screen, almost petting Monique's young face. She'd been with Destiny all that time?

A lump rose in her throat at Monique's demise, at Finn's knife, at the sheer waste of it all.

Libby Knox.

That was a new name.

With Haysle's luck, this Libby woman would already be dead, but she went looking for her anyway, and she found her, surprisingly, only a few hours' drive away.

Haysle opted not to call her. She didn't like calling people on the phone, because of her deep voice, which led to her being misgendered and the awkwardness it always caused. Besides, showing up on a person's doorstep was often more effective.

That night, she rolled over in their new bed and placed her palm on Liam's chest.

He turned to look at her, stifling a yawn.

"I know you're masturbating in the shower and thinking about him," she said.

He let out a noise, something strangled.

"It's all right," she said. "I don't mind. But I know you, Liam, and I'm betting that *you* mind."

He didn't say anything. He seemed to be having trouble breathing.

"If you've been keeping your hands off of me because you think I'm not ready—"

"You're not."

"I think I would know," she said matter-of-factly. "I'm fine. I even want you. But—"

"*I'm* not ready," he muttered.

She caressed his chest, soothing him. "All right. Well, when you are…"

He let out a harsh sounding laugh.

"If you want to talk about Finn, I'm here to listen."

"Why are you being like this? You hate him."

"I want to kill him," she said, still matter-of-fact. "But he told me a long time ago that you and him are a package deal." Her hand moved through his chest hair. "And it seems to be the case in a lot of ways." She had other things to tell him, but not yet. First, she needed to talk to Libby Knox, and then… well, it would probably lead nowhere, but maybe it would be that last bit of reassurance she needed.

"I want to kill him, too," said Liam.

"Liam, it's all right—"

"I do," said Liam, his voice dropping in pitch.

"But you don't hate him."

Liam let out another harsh laugh. "I guess that's not exactly the right word."

"It's okay," she said again. Her hand went lower, down his stomach.

"Haysle." His voice was guttural. A warning.

Her fingers crawled over the slight swell of his belly.

"I just… I just took a shower. I'm spent."

"Are you?" She rubbed gently over his pajama pants, over his crotch.

He let out a grunt.

"Isn't it good somehow, if it's all in the open? The three of us?"

"It's not… he will never touch you again. I *promise* you that." But his cock was stiffening against her.

"Do you like to think about that, though? Us together like you were with Destiny?" Her hand darted under his pants to wrap around his bare, hard girth. "Or maybe *I'm* the middle?"

"Stop that," he said.

Her hand stilled.

"No, don't stop," he said. "I didn't mean it."

She stroked him. "So, would you be in my pussy or my

ass?"

"Fuck, Haysle," he groaned.

Her hand quickened its motion.

Abruptly, he rolled onto her, pinning her into the mattress. He was kissing her—pitiless, brutal kisses, and she wrapped her legs around his hips and arched her torso against his chest.

"He will never touch you again," he breathed into her mouth. "Never."

"No, not really," she gasped. "But it's only pretend. It's safe… tiger."

His pelvis jerked against her. "Fuck," he said again.

"Don't keep things from me, Liam, do you understand me?" she said.

"Yeah," he said. His hands were inside her pajama shirt. "I won't."

"I can handle it. I *want* it."

"Yes," he whispered. "Yes, you do."

CHAPTER TWENTY-ONE

HAYSLE GOT TO Libby Knox's house and circled the place three times in her car.

Then she pulled over, parked, adjusted the rearview mirror, and applied lipstick.

Then she rubbed it off.

Her heart was pounding.

This was wrong. She wasn't this, anymore. She wasn't Detective Dawson. Detective Dawson had drowned in the toilet. Who did Haysle think was going to do this? Who was living inside this body of hers that could interrogate a person?

She hunched down in her seat and gazed at the house.

The house was hidden behind an overgrown yard—maybe better termed a garden because there were so many wildflowers and tangled plants straining against the fence that surrounded it.

There was one clear path to the doorway, a stone walkway, and the house behind it was only one story, and the roof was black metal, but Haysle could not see the siding of the house for the overgrowth to know what color it was.

She put the keys back in the car and started it.

She drove away.

She had driven an hour back toward Cape Christopher when her phone rang. It was Liam.

"Felix called. He set up an interview with Moore, and it's

this evening."

"That's short notice," said Haysle.

"Well, I could have pushed it back, but I feel like we've been waiting forever for this. I want it done. Felix and I have all the information we need, and Moore's going to drop it."

"What time?" she said. "I'm on the road."

"Yeah, what are you up to today again?"

She licked her lips. "Uh… I need to find out about Cora Manning. Not because I have any doubts about you, Liam, but because I just need to know how it happened. I'm, um, I've tracked down a woman from Destiny's group back then, the ones who did the bonfires, and I'm going to go talk to her." She was taking an exit just then, actually. She was turning around. She was going back.

"Oh," said Liam.

"I'm sorry I didn't tell you." Why *hadn't* she told him? Well, it wasn't actually true, what she'd said to him. She *did* have doubts about him. She had doubts about him and Finn and what the two had done together. But she wasn't going to say that out loud. She wished she hadn't even *thought* it in that way. "I don't know why I have to know. It really won't matter, whatever happened."

"I thought you just said—"

"There's something else I should tell you."

"Look, when you get back, before the meeting with Moore—"

"Would you mind terribly if I wasn't there?"

"Oh," he said again.

"It's only that I'm not sure I'll make it back by evening. I've got a lot of driving." One hour there, another hour to talk, three hours back… It all added up to her getting back late.

"I see."

"If I'd had more notice—"

"Haysle, I did not *actually* strangle Cora Manning." His voice was tight.

"I know," she said. "It's a false memory. Destiny put it there."

"You're the one who said that it was me and you, that you would depend on me and I would depend on you."

"It *is* me and you," she said. "It doesn't matter, like I said."

"If it didn't matter, you wouldn't be doing this," he said. "What do you think you're going to find out from this woman? How is she going to know? If Finn and I did do it, then we're the only ones who would have witnessed it, right?"

"Well, obviously, I'm hoping you didn't do it. Trina said that it was at a bonfire. In that garage, before she shot herself, she said, 'I delivered her to the bonfire.'"

"Well, there you go," said Liam. "There you go. Why do you need more than that?"

"I don't know."

Silence.

"Can you just come home?"

"Top right hand drawer in the bathroom off our bedroom?" she said.

"What's that about?"

"What time is your meeting with Moore?"

"Haysle…" He sighed heavily. "Six o'clock."

"I'll do my best, Liam. I love you, okay?"

"Yeah, I love you, too. Just…" Another sigh.

"I'll do my best," she said again. And then she hung up the phone.

When she got back to Libby Knox's house, she got out of the car and ran up the walkway before she could second guess herself again.

At the door, she was sweating. Her heart was beating far too fast. She knocked anyway.

The door opened and the person who answered was a woman who looked to be in her early forties. She had long curly hair, a sort of honey color, and she was wearing a black dress with lace-trimmed bell sleeves. Her voice came out throaty and cigarette-ravaged. "Something I can do for you?"

"A-are you…" Haysle cleared her throat. "That is, um,

I'm looking for Libby Knox."

"You found her." Libby's lips curved into a smile.

"I, um, I'm a private detective," Haysle lied. "I've been hired by the family of a woman named Cora Manning, and my search led me to you. I'm hoping you might know something about what happened to her."

Libby let out a breath. "Wow. Heavy blast from the past."

"I want you to understand that the family doesn't know your name and they made it clear to me that I should give anyone I found every reassurance that they have no intention of pursuing anything against anyone who may have been involved in… in anything untoward with regards to their daughter. They just want to know what happened."

Libby laughed. She reached down the front of her dress and tugged a pack of cigarettes out of her cleavage. "Oh, really? I guess, though, if I don't cooperate with you now, you'll be happy to turn my name over to the police?"

"I didn't say anything like that." Haysle squared her shoulders. "Honestly, all I need from you is just confirmation that Destiny Worth—Lola Gem—that she did it. I need to know there wasn't anyone else involved."

"All *you* need from me? Or all Cora Manning's family needs?"

Haysle looked away.

Libby lit a cigarette and tucked the pack away. "Well, what are the odds you go away if I try to shut this door on you?"

"Slim to none," said Haysle.

Libby chuckled. She backed away from the door. "Then by all means, come in."

Haysle stepped inside the house. It smelled cloyingly of incense and cigarette smoke. There was a Buddha statue on a table just inside the door, surrounded by nubs of candles.

Libby strode ahead of her, smoking, the lace-trimmed sleeves of her dress billowing out with the smoke.

Haysle followed.

They stepped through a beaded curtain and emerged into a kitchen with an old yellow refrigerator. A pot on the stove was boiling and Libby turned down the heat, picking up a wooden spoon to stir the contents. It smelled of garlic and bay leaves. Probably some kind of soup.

"Look, I want you to understand something," said Libby. "I'm not afraid of jail or the cops or anything like that. I am fucking afraid of Lola, though. Lola is a straight-up psycho."

"Lola's dead," said Haysle.

Libby blinked at her. "What?"

Haysle nodded. "Dead. Stabbed in the neck. Her body is in an FBI lab."

Libby's lips parted. "Holy shit, are you serious?"

"It just happened a few weeks ago," said Haysle.

Libby stirred her soup. Ash from her cigarette fell into the pot, and she swore and fished it out with her wooden spoon. She turned back to Haysle, pointing at her with the spoon. "So, I didn't know at the time about Cora, but she was apparently pregnant, and she wouldn't get an abortion, and Lola was mad about this because of whoever the father of the baby was. I got the real impression that Lola had a thing for this guy, and that she was somehow, uh, jealous of Cora. But like I said, not at the time. At the time, Lola just did the sacrifice the way we always did it, which was with stuff put in the person's drink so that they'd pass out, and then we, uh…" Libby's voice broke. "We smothered her." She looked away, back to her soup, and her body trembled.

"You did it? You witnessed it?"

"It's weird the things you can do that you didn't think you could do. Like, I remember hearing about the Manson family or even more recently, that, uh, that place not that far from here in West Virginia, the Fellowship of the Children of the Lord? Where they killed the little boy? When I heard about that shit, I always thought it was crazy. How could another person convince someone to do something like that?" She sucked on her cigarette. "And then, there I was, chanting shit about love and sacrifice and holding a pillow over a person's face."

"Good," said Haysle, letting out a breath.

Libby looked up at her, shaking her head. "What?"

"And, um, you said that the father of Cora's baby… you never met him?"

"No, I don't know who he was. I never even knew his name, but after all this, one night, Lola was going off about this guy, about Cora, and I remember Trina—that's Cora's sister, did you talk to her?"

"Trina Manning is dead too." *She blew her head off right in front of my face.*

"Seriously?" Libby stubbed her cigarette out in an ashtray.

"You were saying?"

"Trina got angry with Lola about it. And then she left, and I didn't last much longer after that either." She fished out her pack of cigarettes. "Why do you think that is, huh? Why couldn't I stop myself from smothering people, but then I could somehow leave? How does that make sense?" She was bitter.

"It's not your fault," said Haysle. "She, um, she had a way of breaking people down."

"I guess," said Libby, shrugging.

"One more question," said Haysle. "Did you ever meet someone named Liam Emerson?"

Libby furrowed her brow. "That sounds familiar." She lifted her chin. "Oh, wait, isn't he somehow connected with that Phineas Slater person, the guy who was at our college right at that same time, the serial killer? I followed the news about that, you know, and he escaped again."

"So, you didn't know them when you were going to Branwen College?"

"No. No, never spoke to that Slater person. I wasn't aware that Emerson person went to Branwen. I thought he was just kept in some dog crate in a bunker. That wasn't that far away from here, actually."

"But you had no connection with them then, and neither did Cora. And you saw her die?"

"What is this really about?"

"Nothing," said Haysle, shaking her head. "Nothing." *Everything.* She crossed the kitchen and took one of Libby's hands in both of her own. "Thank you. I know this can't have been easy to talk about. That's all I needed from you."

"Are you really a private detective?"

"Yes," said Haysle, nodding. "But you have nothing to fear from admitting this to me, I promise you. And you won't hear from me again." She gestured. "I'll see myself out."

When she got back to her car, she glanced into the back seat, because she always did that, after that time that she and Liam had gotten into the car and Finn had been in the back, waiting for them.

It was empty.

But then she made sure to lock her car these days, something she never used to worry about before all this happened. In fact, working robbery, she used to leave her car unlocked precisely because she didn't want to deal with the damage that came from someone breaking into a car to steal a stereo. She'd much rather have a drivable car with no stereo than a broken window.

She fished the car keys out of her pocket and pressed the button to unlock the car.

Movement.

Out of the corner of her eye.

She whirled.

Finn's hand covered her mouth, his lips moved against her cheekbone. "Hi there, Haysle."

CHAPTER TWENTY-TWO

LIAM SPENT TOO long in the bathroom with the drawer open, staring at what was inside it. Well, first, he didn't understand it, so he had to get out his phone and look it up online, and then he stared at it, and then he thought about it, and then he cried.

It was funny, because he hadn't cried a lot about all of it.

Even what had happened to Haysle, as awful as that was, it hadn't really induced a significant teary session.

But this.

He wept.

It went on for too long.

He wasn't really over it when he went to meet Felix at the Cape Christopher Police Department.

Haysle wasn't there.

He should have called her. Should have called her while he was weeping. Should have said the things to her, the *right* things. He felt the right things about it, at least he thought he did.

Instead, he just told Felix that Haysle had gotten stuck in traffic and that she'd get there as soon as she could, and they walked into the police station, and he still felt tears threatening when his thoughts strayed back to everything that had happened that afternoon.

When they arrived in the interrogation room, Captain Moore wasn't there, only Mitch Clark was.

"The captain's wife took a bad fall down some stairs, and he's with her," said Clark.

"Oh, God," said Liam.

"She's maybe broken her leg," said Clark, "but she's fine. She's going to be fine."

"You could have called us," said Felix. "We'll reschedule."

"It's all going to be recorded," said Clark. "I'm running this show here, anyway. I'm the one who's been doing all the legwork."

"Let's get it over with," said Liam, leveling his gaze at Clark.

So, they sat down, and Clark wasn't certain of anything. He said he was confused about a lot of things, that he found Ricky's statements contradictory and unconvincing, and when Felix started dropping receipts and CCTV footage of Liam — printed out as glossy photos with time stamps — all over the table, Clark pulled away from it, swallowing hard as he surveyed the evidence.

The meeting didn't last too much longer after that.

Clark didn't say that it was all over, but Liam could see that he was shaken by the proof that he'd never been at Finn's murder scenes, and that he wasn't going to pursue it.

Liam just wasn't sure why Clark was so shaken.

In the parking lot, he and Felix shook hands and he watched the lawyer drive off. When he looked back over at his own car, Clark was sauntering over, hands in his pockets.

Shit.

Liam looked around. They were in the parking lot outside the police station, for fuck's sake. Why did he feel a sharp stab of panic about this?

He took a deep breath and approached Clark, feeling as if he were steeling himself for battle. "You want to talk, detective?" he called.

Clark closed in on him. "I'm guessing you're not a murderer, Emerson."

Well, you'd be wrong about that. "Nope," he said cheerily.

"And I think it's pretty obvious it would be stupid for the department to waste resources on you," said Clark.

"I feel like there's a 'but' coming." *Don't taunt him, Liam, for God's sake.*

"But," said Clark with an ironic smile, "I don't like you."

Liam barked out a laugh. "What?"

"I don't know what it is," said Clark, looking him over. "You're not good for Haysle Dawson, either."

Told you I'd be bad for you, Haysle.

"I don't think this is any of your business, detective."

"If she ever indicates to me that you've hurt her in any way—"

"You don't even know Haysle. Where's this big brother shit coming from?" Liam shoved his own hands into his pockets, mimicking Clark's posture.

"Someone's got to look out for her. I consider her a friend and a colleague, that's all." Clark's smile deepened. "Just want you to know I'm watching you."

Fucking macho bullshit. "Is that all?" Liam raised his eyebrows. Suddenly, in his pocket, his phone was ringing. He yanked it out. It was Haysle. He lifted a finger to Clark, answering it, putting it to his ear. "Hello?"

But there was no answer on the other end, just distant voices, both of which were deep.

"Where are you taking me, Finn?" That was Haysle's voice.

Liam stiffened, clutching the phone.

"Just drive and I'll tell you when to turn, Haysle. Be a good girl now."

"Why? What are you planning on doing to me?"

"What's with the questi—" Suddenly Finn's voice was much louder. "Well, well, well, look at you. Dialing when I wasn't watching."

"He's at the police station right now, Finn. It is over. They are going to track this phone, and you are—"

"She's going to eat for me, tiger," said Finn's voice, so loud Liam jerked the phone away from his ear. "She's going to eat for me, and then I'm going to kill her, and then I'm going to fuck her mouth and then her ass and then her pussy, and you are never going to see her again, because you're *mine*." The line went dead.

Liam pulled the phone away from his ear, and he whimpered. Tears were in his eyes again.

"What the fuck?" said Clark, eyes wide. "Was that Slater?"

Liam nodded. "We have to stop him."

"Oh, I'm bagging that bastard," said Clark. He held out his hand for the phone. "Let's get her number and trace that phone."

HAYSLE SLAMMED ON the brakes.

"What are you doing?" Finn slapped her across the face.

She gritted her teeth. "You think I'm doing *anything* you say? You're going to kill me. What does it matter? I'm not cooperating." She had the thing she could tell him. That would stop him. But she didn't want to tell him. She didn't want him to know.

"I'm not going to kill you."

"You just told Liam that—"

"I just said that," said Finn. "I wouldn't kill you, Haysle."

She laughed. Abruptly, she yanked the keys out of the ignition and threw open the door.

Finn lunged for her.

She collided with the pavement—hard against her shoulder—pain like bright sparks—and she rolled and scrambled to her feet and ran.

He dove out after her, leaving the car in the middle of the road, driver's side door open, dome light burning.

She ran across the other lane and leaped over the guardrail and began to clamber down the hill on the other side.

It was dark. Early evening in the late fall. She couldn't see where she was going, but she needed to find a house. She needed to get—

Finn slammed into her from behind.

They went down, her chin skidding painfully into the ground.

He turned her body, taking her by the shoulders, slamming her against the ground again and again. "I'll just do it now. I don't need the ritual. I need you gone. You took him from me."

"Fuck you," she spat in his face. "He'll never choose you, Finn. You're not what he wants. He wants someone who can care about him, and you—"

Finn wrapped his hands around her neck.

Her breath was immediately cut off.

She drove the keys up into his midsection.

He cried out, grasping her hand, squeezing it painfully until he got the keys out of her hand. He shoved them into his pocket, and then he put his hand back to where his other one was, around her neck, and redoubled his squeezing efforts.

She struggled, striking his hands, wriggling her body.

It was no good. He was too strong for her. He was going to choke the life out of her here on the side of the road in the dark and she couldn't talk, so she couldn't even tell him the thing.

She bucked with her hips.

No, not my hips!

She brought up her knee, right into his groin.

He loosened his grip, crying out in rage.

"I'm pregnant."

He tightened his grip, but not tight enough to stop her breath.

"It's yours."

CHAPTER TWENTY-THREE

LIAM HAD TAKEN the pregnancy test from the top drawer in the upstairs bathroom, which might be a gross thing to have done, considering it had Haysle's dried urine on it, but he liked to think they were beyond these sorts of things between them.

Now, as he was standing in the police station, waiting on the trace on Haysle's phone, he felt around for it in his pocket. It was in a plastic baggy and it crinkled when he took it out and looked at it. He had known, when he found it, that it must be positive, because who kept a negative pregnancy test?

But he had googled it anyway, just to make sure he was right, because he needed to be certain.

And the weeping, it wasn't all sorrow.

Some of it was.

After all, how did she get so unlucky as all that? He and Haysle had sex without protection a zillion times—well, he was exaggerating, but it had been a lot—and she'd gotten her period anyway, and then Finn... once. Just like that.

She hated Finn, and she had been violated, and for that to have happened to her, it wasn't fair. It was too much, too much for Haysle.

But some of the weeping had been hope and happiness, because there it was. They'd wanted it, and there it was. A baby.

He didn't know, of course, maybe Haysle wouldn't want to keep it, and he would utterly support her if that was the case. He could understand why she might not want to.

But he and Haysle were in sync in a way that they hadn't been before their stint with Destiny, and he was almost entirely certain she'd keep it, and she'd told him about it and kept the pregnancy test because she still wanted him part of it, and he wanted that too.

None of his sorrow was for him.

He didn't care, he found, if it was Finn's sperm or his that had made that baby in Haysle, because it just didn't matter, and… maybe it some ways, it was sort of poetic. Maybe it was even good. Maybe it made up for what he'd already decided he had to do.

The timetable had been moved up, however.

He'd been waiting.

He'd been nervous and hesitant.

But it had to be now.

There was no way he could risk waiting any longer.

"What's that you got?" It was Clark's voice.

"Uh, nothing." Liam tried to put the pregnancy test back in his pocket, but he was clumsy, and it slipped from his fingers. He dropped it.

Clark swooped down and picked it up. He furrowed his brow and handed it back to Liam.

Liam did shove it in his pocket.

"Dawson?" said Clark. "Can she, um, do that?"

"She didn't have any surgeries when she transitioned," said Liam.

Clark swallowed. "Well, that just makes everything worse, doesn't it?"

"No," said Liam. "She'll tell him. He won't hurt her."

Clark raised his eyebrows. "You think he's got moral lines he doesn't cross? Really?"

"It's, uh, it's his," said Liam in a low voice.

"What?" Clark's voice was shrill.

"I think she told you that when we were captured—"

"Yeah, well, she's never given us a statement."

"Well, we don't need it to put him away," said Liam. "We've got enough evidence to give Finn the death penalty over and over again."

"Damned shame it takes so long to kill a fuck like him," muttered Clark.

Liam nodded. He was in agreement at this point. There was a time when some part of him still wanted Finn alive, but that part of him had been stabbed in the neck along with Destiny.

"Still, is that really going to stop him?"

"When he found out about Cora Manning being pregnant with his kid, it really affected him. Yeah, he'll stop."

Clark let out a breath. "Well, that's relieving. We got the phone's coordinates, but it's been sitting still for the past twenty minutes."

"He tossed it out of the window when he found out Haysle had it," said Liam.

"Let me show you where it is on the map," said Clark, getting out his own phone, and clicking on the screen. He handed it over. "Which direction do you think he's going?"

Liam shook his head. "He wouldn't be so stupid as to go to the cabin, would he?"

"That's where all the original murders took place."

"It's where he kept me in the dog crate," said Liam. "In the bunker." He pointed. "It's probably a half hour away from these coordinates."

"But he knows we'd look for him there."

"Yeah, it's really a stupid move," said Liam.

"But I'll swing by there on my way to the coordinates," said Clark. "I've got a swarm of uniforms coming with me, too, but I'm asking them to go stealth until we know we have him. I don't want to spook him with sirens and everything else." He held out his hand for his phone.

"Wait, I'm coming with you," said Liam.

Clark snorted, snatching back his phone. "The fuck you are." He took off walking down the hallway.

Liam went after him. "You need me. I can help. No one knows Finn better than me."

"Look, even if you were actually still a consultant to this department—and you're officially not anymore, by the way—I would not take you, because you're way too close to this emotionally. You can't go after your *girlfriend*. It's not professional."

Liam caught up to him. "Nothing about this case is professional at this point."

"No."

"I know where the damned cabin is," said Liam. "I'll just go there myself. I'm going with or without you, Clark."

"I should have you taken into custody for your own good."

"I will call my lawyer if you even think about it, and—"

"I'm not going to waste time on that." Clark pushed open the front door of the station, going out into the darkness and chill of the evening. "I got to get to Dawson."

"Take me with you," said Liam, keeping pace with him.

Clark sighed heavily. "Fine. I can't believe I'm agreeing to this."

"Thank you," said Liam.

"I still don't like you," said Clark.

"Yeah, fine," said Liam. "We can save her and stop Finn and not like each other."

Clark let out a wondering laugh. "Oh, man, nothing like this ever used to *happen* in Cape Christopher."

FINN TOWERED OVER Haysle, face solemn and barely visible in the darkness.

She scrambled to her feet, warily looking at him.

"You're lying," he said.

"I'm not," she said. "You threw my phone away, but I had a picture of a pregnancy test on it. I took it only five days ago."

"That wouldn't prove anything anyway," said Finn. "You were already pregnant, because Liam said that was why we had to get you out of the hole at Destiny's. It's Liam's kid."

"It's not," she said. "I got my period when I was there. You're the only person I had sex with until, well, two nights ago."

"You're lying," said Finn firmly.

"What if I'm not?"

His nostrils flared. He snatched her by the arm. "You're *lying*."

"You keep saying that, but it doesn't change the fact that I am gestating your goddamned spawn."

He leaned down eye level with her, baring his teeth. "Don't call it that."

She gave him a nasty smile. "Oh, struck a nerve? I still remember how you almost *cried* when we told you Cora Manning was preggo with Finn Junior."

"Shut up," he snarled, pushing her ahead of him back up the hill.

She let out a wild and ragged laugh. "You can't chance it, Finn. Imagine knowing that you killed the mother of your child while the baby was still inside her. Imagine how that would make you feel."

He pressed into her from behind. "Walk, bitch. I couldn't give a fuck about you or whatever is in your womb. I *will* kill you."

She went cold all over.

"I need to do it for Liam," he said. "Liam is more important to me than... than..." He shoved her. "*Walk.*"

She walked.

When they got to the road, a car was swerving around their car, blaring their horn at the abandoned vehicle.

He shoved her into the driver's seat. "You're going to drive."

"And if I say no?" She looked up at him defiantly. They couldn't be very far from the place where Finn had thrown the phone out of the window. How long would it take for them to trace her number and get the coordinates? Twenty minutes? A half hour?

Oh, but then it would probably take them at least an hour to drive here.

No, maybe it was a losing proposition to be too defiant. Maybe she should cooperate. She put her hands on the steering wheel, and she felt like crying. "Fine."

He shut the door on her.

She wished she still had the keys. If she did, she could just drive off without him.

He climbed in beside her.

A car appeared behind them, going fast, headlights flooding everything.

Her heart stuttered. It was going to run into them. She reached for the door handle, ready to bail, letting out a little cry.

The car swerved around them, laying on the horn as the last one had done.

She let out a breathy noise of relief.

He put the keys in the ignition and cranked it. "Drive."

She drove.

"I KNEW HIM, you know?" Clark was saying as he drove through the night. "We worked together in homicide for years. I considered him a friend."

Sometimes Liam forgot how Finn used to be a police officer at the Cape Christopher department, how he'd actually engineered his own demise, calling in the help of the Wren Delacroix and Caius Reilly team who seemed to catch one serial killer every year and who had clocked Finn immediately.

Finn had captured them and they'd all been locked up in that bunker together, the place they were returning to, the dark hole where Liam's nightmares sometimes lived. But the truth was, Liam's life had been a trip from one nightmare to the next, and all of them had been entwined with Finn.

"Yeah, he can be really friendly when he wants to be," said Liam.

"Charming is the word I'd use," said Clark.

"Really?"

"That surprises you?" said Clark. "We never would have suspected him, you know, because he was gay, and the victims were all women."

"But they weren't, though," said Liam. "Because he started branching out."

"Yeah, at the end, he killed a man and a trans woman, but before that, they were all women. And anyway, I'm a straight man myself, but I'll admit that Slater had a… a thing about him."

Liam just regarded Clark, unsure of what to say.

"I mean, you obviously know what I'm talking about," said Clark.

"I don't know if I do," said Liam.

"This is why I don't like you," said Clark.

"Okay," said Liam.

"This is not an easy thing for me to talk about, really. I wouldn't share this with Moore or anything. He'd think… I'm just saying, there are ways that a man can charm another man, without my wanting, you know… to have a thing with him. I still could be charmed."

Liam supposed he did understand, but he was about done with Clark's no-homo caveats to the whole thing. "Okay, sure."

"What do you mean by that?"

"I'm only saying that I understand what it is you're saying."

"No, your tone was not saying that."

"You know I'm bisexual."

"Yeah?"

"Well…" Liam leaned his head back against the headrest of the car. "I know it's typical for people of all situations to graft themselves onto other individuals and assume that their subjective experiences are universal, so it's possible that I'm just wrong, but I kind of don't even believe in sexual orientation."

"What?" Clark made a dismissive noise. "You can't be serious."

"I think people have, you know, a type," he said. "And

that type probably has a gender. But I think given the right circumstances, anyone will fuck anything."

Clark made the dismissive noise again.

Liam began to tick things off on his fingers. "Case in point, the Roman army. Case in point, prison. Case in point, all of Joe Exotic's straight husbands."

Clark laughed out loud.

Liam found himself smirking a bit too.

"You're funny, Emerson," said Clark.

"I'm not trying to be."

"Those are extreme circumstances," said Clark.

"Well, you'd have sex with a man in extreme circumstances, too, that's all I'm saying." He shifted in his seat.

Clark glanced at him. "Okay, now you're—"

"And you might even like it," said Liam, looking out the window in the darkness.

"I really, really don't like you," said Clark.

Liam grinned. "Yeah, you keep saying that."

CHAPTER TWENTY-FOUR

HAYSLE COULDN'T BELIEVE Finn was having her drive back to the cabin where he'd committed all his original murders. Was he really that stupid, or did he just want to get caught?

If she'd been feeling more secure in her chances of survival, she might have taunted him, but she kept her mouth shut.

Finn talked instead.

He babbled a long time about the first time he met Liam, and how he had never met anyone like Liam before, and how Liam had fascinated him for his entire life, and how she had stolen Liam from Finn and how she was going to pay for that.

She didn't say anything to counter this, either, because she couldn't believe he was being so incredibly pathetic.

However, that seemed to be the truth of this man.

When he'd been locked up in prison, and she'd gone to visit him and tried to get information about Destiny Worth, he'd been a paradox—lethal and influential, able to bend her to his will and force her to obey his orders about buying and eating fast food, and also a sad and pitiful man who had often seemed to have the emotional maturity of a toddler and who had been hurt and sad a lot of the time.

It was hard not to feel bad for him, even though she knew what he was.

That was the thing that people didn't get about serial killers, she supposed. Those women who became pen pals with them, they were drawn to that sad, kicked puppy side to the men. They always seemed to have it, or maybe they faked it, maybe it was all one big manipulation.

But she didn't think Finn was faking this.

He was really just this way. He didn't know how to love other people. He seemed incapable of it, in fact. And yet, he craved the love of others, just like any other human being.

That was his tragedy, she supposed.

But she didn't really care about Finn, or how sad or tragic he might be. She cared about precisely one thing and that was to get out of this alive and to save her baby.

She had known there was a baby before the pregnancy test, known it because she'd been waiting anxiously for her period since getting away from Destiny. While being there, she'd lost track of time, but when she was free, she had been able to see that she should have had her cycle again since Finn had raped her.

She told herself that she'd probably just been starved to the point of amenorrhea. Surely, once she started eating again and putting on weight, her period would come back. But it didn't. And then she started feeling nausea in the mornings, just a light bit of nausea.

Still, she didn't take the test, because she wasn't sure how she felt about it.

She felt as though she should feel angry and disgusted. She and Liam had planned to have a baby together, and this wasn't her plan. She should also be concerned, because Finn was supremely fucked up and who knew if carrying on his genes was a particularly good thing.

But she mostly felt excited about the idea, because finally—*finally*—after everything she'd been through, she was pregnant.

And that seemed… wrong to her.

It was the idea of having a baby that had caused her to detransition in the first place. She and Carter had decided it was stupid to adopt when she had a functioning womb, and she'd gone off hormones in the pursuit of getting back her cycle and getting pregnant. But somewhere in the middle of it all, she'd known she couldn't go back, that she didn't want to take testosterone anymore, and that she wanted to keep her softer, rounder body, that she wanted the baby she carried to call her "Mom," that she wanted to be a woman again.

It had been painful but undeniable, and now, here she was, and it was going to happen.

She felt... it was stupid... she had been born female and she had always had female genitals and breasts, and yet... this was the first time she'd felt *really* female in her entire life.

She liked it.

She had to forgive herself for liking it before she could take the pregnancy test. Somewhere in the middle of that was when she forgave Liam for liking sex with Finn. She didn't know why either of them were the way they were, and she knew they were both badly messed up in the head, but she didn't care.

She was already in love with the baby, that was the thing.

That love that Finn craved, she felt it for his child, and she didn't care if the baby did have terrible psychopathy genes scrambled into its DNA. None of that mattered. She didn't know why. Maybe that was screwed up too.

But maybe she was just fine with being screwed up. Just exactly fine with it.

They pulled up to the cabin and he told her to park.

She did and he reached over and took the keys out of the ignition as if he was afraid she was going to try to get them and use them as a weapon again.

Not that her first attempt had been very effective, admittedly.

This made her realize he seemed to have captured her with no weapons whatsoever.

If she'd had her gun, if she hadn't been on suspension—

Should have just bought a gun, she thought. Open carry was legal for anyone in Virginia who was over the age of eighteen years old. She could have had a firearm strapped to her at any and all times. Why had she not simply done that?

Hindsight was twenty-twenty, of course.

He opened the door to the car and got out.

She stayed where she was.

He came around and opened her door.

She looked up at him. "Why here?"

He hauled her up out of the car.

"You want to get caught, don't you?" she said.

He dragged her along with him and she struggled to keep up. They walked past the cabin itself and out into the field, where the entrance to the bunker was.

"Maybe you've wanted to get caught all along," she said.

"I'm not going back to jail," he said.

She laughed. "What do you think's going to happen?"

"Liam's coming," he said softly. "Liam's coming. I need him to find me. I'd rather you didn't talk anymore."

She wrenched herself out of his grasp, only managing it because he hadn't been expecting it. She took off running, because what he'd said had terrified her. If he didn't want her to talk, it was because he was psyching himself up to murder her, detaching from her, wanting to turn her into an object, because objects were easier to destroy. Objects didn't talk, and people did. Therefore, he didn't want her to talk.

Finn pivoted and came after her.

She picked up the pace, running back for the cabin, trying to think. *Get to the cabin. Break a window. Use the glass. Cut him.*

It wasn't a great plan, but it was something.

But as she approached the cabin, someone stepped out from around the side of the building, a shadowed figure holding a rifle and a voice rang out. "Freeze."

CHAPTER TWENTY-FIVE

HAYSLE'S FIRST THOUGHT was that she was saved.

The police were here.

They had figured it out and they had driven like bats out of hell—no, they'd called the local guys to come, of *course* they'd done that, and the local police department was here with—

But then the figure came closer and Haysle recognized it as Mick.

The man from the gate, the one that had turned her over to Finn to be raped for the price of a cigarette.

Her knees buckled and she fell down to the ground, just out of the sheer awfulness of him being here.

How could he—?

"We knew you'd show up eventually," Mick was saying, pointing the end of the barrel at Finn.

Other people were coming out of the shadows, and Destiny recognized Kyleigh and Pam and other members of Destiny's cult. They yanked her to her feet and zip-tied her hands behind her back, securing Finn the same way. They all seemed to have guns—pistols and rifles and shotguns—and they herded them off into the woods where they had a minivan with the backseats removed.

"Into the back," said Mick, gesturing with the gun.

Finn was seething. "Just shoot me."

"No," said Mick. "Not yet. We need to release the power

you stole from Destiny."

"The highest form of love is sacrifice," said Kyleigh.

"You are the sacrifice," said one of the others. "Phineas Slater."

"Wait," spoke up Haysle. "Wait, why don't you just let me go? He's the one who killed Destiny. I didn't do it. You don't even want me."

They shoved them both into the back of the van, prodding them with their guns.

Then everyone climbed into the van, the rest of them crammed into the remaining seats.

The van sped off into the night, and when they got onto the main road, they went past a number of police cars, all traveling without their sirens, stealthily heading towards the cabin.

Too late, thought Haysle. She tried to bang on the window and get the attention of the police, but she couldn't make much noise without use of her hands, and someone from up front gestured with the gun for her to sit down.

"We don't need you for the sacrifice," said Pam. "We could just shoot you now if we need to."

Haysle ducked down, gritting her teeth. She didn't try again.

LIAM RAN HIS fingers over the steering wheel of Haysle's car.

The place was now swarming with cops, and they had looked everywhere. In the cabin, in the bunker, in the surrounding woods.

No one was here.

No sign of anyone, except the car.

What was going on?

Clark approached from the darkness, holding a flashlight that danced and bounced ahead of him. "I just heard from the guys who've recovered Dawson's phone. It's by the side of the road, no sign of them."

"Well, that's what we figured," said Liam. "Besides, the car's here. They came here."

"They must have switched vehicles," said Clark. "Slater had a car here. There's some freshly pushed-down grass we found. Looks like maybe a van. Actually, a few of the squad cars remember seeing one go through, and we got something on one of the squad car's cameras. So, we're running plates now."

Liam swallowed. "Okay, that's good."

"Well, it's something, but it's honestly not great," said Clark. "I mean, we can maybe get footage from cameras on the interstate, but if he's intent on doing harm to her tonight, we're going to be too late."

"He won't," said Liam.

"You think he intended to kill her here and run after, but he took her with him because she told him about the pregnancy?"

"It makes sense," said Liam. But he was starting to feel ill, because he didn't know what Finn would do. Some part of him had hoped Finn would just let Haysle go once he knew about the baby. The fact he'd taken her along with him didn't bode well.

A uniformed officer approached. "Detective Clark? We've got a hit on the plates. They're registered to someone named Mick Donovan."

Liam straightened, eyes widening. What the hell? That didn't make *any* sense.

HAYSLE GOT CARSICK in the back of the van, or maybe it was because of her pregnancy, because she had discovered that if she wasn't vigilant about eating, her nausea was exacerbated. She vomited in a corner of the van, getting it in her hair, and Kyleigh swore at her and clubbed her over the head with the butt of her rifle.

"Don't," growled Finn. "She's pregnant."

This little bit of triumph that she felt at his protecting her was short lived, because what did it really matter if they were just going to be sacrificed by the remaining members of Destiny's cult?

Haysle got sick relatively early in the journey, and they were all stuck smelling the vomit for the rest of the drive, which was miserable and long.

She watched out the window and eventually realized that they were heading to Delaware. They skirted the edge of Branwen College and went down a country road, and she realized they were going back to the house where the bonfires had happened, the place where she and Liam had found the freezer full of dead bodies.

Well.

This was good.

This was an obvious place for them to go to.

Liam would figure it out, and as soon as he did, he'd call *this* local police department, and she'd be rescued.

Except Liam wouldn't figure it out, because he'd have no idea that the cult had captured them and he'd never know to associate it with this place, which had no significance to Finn and only had significance to Destiny.

She and Slater were deposited on the ground outside and the others began to busy themselves making a bonfire.

A member of the cult named Brenda was watching them, but she had her rifle slung over her shoulder and Haysle thought that if she tackled the woman, Brenda would never get the gun out and cocked in time to shoot them.

But with her hands zip-tied behind her back, Haysle didn't see what good it would be to get Brenda's gun.

Finn nudged himself close to her, and she stiffened and tried to crawl away, but his voice was hot against her ear, barely audible.

"We have to work together now."

CHAPTER TWENTY-SIX

MICK'S CAR.

LIAM couldn't make that work.

Maybe Finn had gone back to steal another car from the cult, and that was why he had Mick's van?

Liam knew that Destiny had been in the habit of getting property registered under the names of her followers, which had made it difficult to track her. They had searched a lot of Worth properties, for instance, and then it had turned out she'd had a deed under another cult member's name, and they never would have found it anyway.

So, the idea that the car was registered to Mick, that didn't mean it was Mick's car, not necessarily. It was cult property.

"What are you thinking?" Clark said to Liam.

"I don't know," he said. "I really don't."

"Well, you reacted to that name, so why don't you tell me what's going on?"

"That was the name of one of Destiny's followers," said Liam. "The first car we had, the one we all escaped in, Finn stole that one from the cult, so maybe he went back and stole another."

"You don't sound sure about that."

"Well, what if Mick were here, I guess?" said Liam.

"Would Mick be here?"

"This cabin was owned by Destiny," said Liam. "She

controlled all of the Worth fortune. She had her father imprisoned in a basement somewhere and she was using other people to do his bidding and business, so it's not as if this property wouldn't have been known to the cult. In fact, when Finn was killing here, he always claimed it was at the behest of Destiny, that she had made him do it."

Clark snorted. "You believe that?"

"Destiny liked to push people," said Liam. "She liked to control people. Finn was a person she could never control, and there wasn't very much you could push him into. But… it could be true. She was killing before he was. We know that's true. So, it's all possible. But I guess it doesn't really matter, not right now."

"No, it doesn't," said Clark. "Why would this Mick person be here?"

Liam shook his head. "Uh… maybe he was trying to escape the cult. Maybe he… God, I have no idea."

"But we don't really have any reason to think he was here."

"No," said Liam.

"If Slater took her, where do you think he would go?"

"Well, he came here, which was a significant place for him. Maybe he'd go some other place that was significant."

"Like where?"

"The only other significant places I can think of are in Delaware," said Liam.

Clark rubbed his forehead.

"I mean, there's the other bunker," said Liam. "If we call the department in Delaware, they'd know what I was talking about. They could send a few officers to check it out, but they're a small town police department. There's probably two guys on duty for the whole town right now, and that against Finn…"

"Okay, well, I'll get in touch with them," said Clark. "And you and I, we're going to Delaware."

Liam let out a breath.

"Unless you think there's somewhere else we should go?"

Liam shook his head. "No, no, I guess not."

HAYSLE WENT STILL against Finn. He was right. Their best bet at getting out of this was to work together, but she couldn't trust him.

"Say you have to pee," came Finn's barely audible voice.

This was his plan?

Haysle swallowed. "We need to get out of the zip-ties."

Brenda came closer. "Did you say something?"

Haysle glared up at her.

Finn nudged her shoulder.

And then Haysle saw it, sticking up out of the pocket of Brenda's jeans. A pocket knife. Haysle squared her shoulders. "I said that I have to pee."

"No one's stopping you," said Brenda.

"Look, I was already trapped with the smell of my own vomit, and I'd rather not be trapped with the smell of my own urine," said Haysle. "If we're dying, can't you give me that much dignity?"

Brenda eyed her.

"I need someone to help me," said Haysle. "I can't get to my button and zipper with my hands behind my back."

Brenda pressed her lips together. "Well, I'm not walking out in the woods with you. You want to take a piss, you do it right here." She gestured with her head to a spot only a few feet away.

"Fine," said Haysle, struggling to her feet, which was very hard to do without use of her hands. She walked over to the spot where Brenda had gestured.

Brenda sighed and came over.

Haysle maneuvered herself to be facing Finn and Brenda put her back to Finn to unbutton Haysle's pants.

Finn moved fast. He leaped into Brenda, knocking her into Haysle, and all three of them went down.

Brenda shrieked, going for the gun.

Haysle rolled onto her stomach, reaching back with her hand for the pocket knife.

"What are you doing, trying to finger me?" Brenda snarled.

Finn slammed his head into Brenda's, and she screamed.

Now, others were coming for them. A shot rang out in the air.

Haysle's fingers closed over the pocket knife and she pulled it out.

"I will shoot you, Phineas," came Mick's voice. "Don't think I won't. All you have to do is be alive long enough for the ritual. Doesn't matter if you're bleeding."

Haysle eased open the pocket knife and cut her zip tie but kept her hands behind her back.

Brenda got to her feet, unslinging her rifle, clutching her head with her other hand. She let out a litany of swear words.

Haysle passed the pocket knife to Finn. She wouldn't have bothered, but she might need him, might need his strength.

Mick was close, pointing a gun at both of them.

Finn smiled up at him. "Well, go on, then. Shoot me."

"I got them," said Brenda, cocking the rifle, pointing it first at Haysle and then at Finn.

Mick put his gun up. "Make sure you watch them, okay?"

"I will," said Brenda.

Mick walked off, going to check the fire and then disappearing into the woods to look for firewood.

Soon enough, they were alone again with Brenda, who was now tense, gritting her teeth as she covered them with the rifle.

Well, now their hands were free, but were they really any better off?

Finn nudged her.

She looked at him, shaking her head. It would be stupid to try something now.

"I think she still has to pee," said Finn.

Brenda let out a snort, raising the gun as she did. "Oh, no way, you think I'm that stup—"

Finn brought down the pocket knife on Brenda's foot.

She pulled the trigger, and the gunshot was loud, but it went over Haysle's head.

Finn sprang up and seized the rifle. He and Brenda fought over it.

"What's going on?" came Mick's voice.

Haysle reached forward and plucked the pocket knife out of Brenda's foot.

This seemed to surprise Brenda, and Finn wrenched the rifle free.

He struggled with the bolt action for a minute but then seemed to understand it. He wrenched everything into place, which caused the gun to spit out the spent cartridge, and then he shot Brenda in the face.

Her body flew backwards, thudding against the ground.

Finn turned on the approaching Mick, who shouted and simultaneously hit the ground, taking cover behind a log that was set up as seat around the fire.

Mick yelled, "Little help here! Phineas has a gun."

"Let's go," said Finn to Haysle, yanking her by the hand. "There's too many of them and they're all armed."

Together, they fled into the woods.

CHAPTER TWENTY-SEVEN

RICKY SET DOWN a bowl of popcorn on the coffee table in his living room.

Tyler leaned forward, grinning, and took a handful, popping kernels in his mouth.

Ricky got a handful himself.

The two chewed, surveying the other.

Ricky wasn't sure what this was between them. Tyler was still sleeping on his couch, and they hadn't so much as held hands, and yet… something was happening, some kind of odd intimacy that was deeper than he was used to.

Earlier that day, Tyler had gotten in touch with his mother, who hadn't seen him in years, and the woman had sobbed over the phone and Tyler's eyes had shimmered as well. It had made Ricky want to tear up, too. Tyler's mother wanted to come and pick him up and take him home with her, but Tyler had hedged, seemingly frightened, and Ricky understood.

He had been talking on the phone with his own parents since getting back, but he hadn't visited them again. It wasn't only because they attacked him for being "crazy" about Destiny, but because something about it was simply overwhelming.

Tyler, though, Tyler felt safe.

Why it was that the man who'd been essentially his jailer for months was the safe one, Ricky didn't know. But he also knew that no matter what Tyler had done, it hadn't been of Tyler's free will. He had been Destiny's tool, just as Ricky had.

Ricky didn't know what would happen next between him and Tyler, but he wanted to find out, so he was willing to be patient and wait. They both had a lot of weirdness to peel back.

"Did you pick a movie?" he asked Tyler.

"You've probably seen it," said Tyler.

"I don't care," said Ricky. Tyler hadn't been allowed to watch a lot of television or movies in the cult. It hadn't been forbidden, per se, but the members didn't have much down time, so there wasn't much time for entertainment.

"You sure, because if you want to pick something else—"

They were interrupted as Ricky's phone began to ring.

Ricky didn't recognize the number. He dismissed it. "We'll watch whatever you want to watch."

"Who was that?" said Tyler.

"I don't know," said Ricky. "They can leave a message."

The phone started to ring again.

Ricky lifted it, and his body went tense.

"Answer it," said Tyler in a low voice.

Ricky put it to his ear. "Hello?"

"It's Liam."

Ricky let out a harsh breath.

"I know you don't want to talk to me," said Liam. "I know that you have false memories that Destiny put in your head, and I have them too, so I know how that is, but even if you didn't, you still shouldn't want to talk to me, because I was definitely a shitty boyfriend to you, and I get that. But don't hang up?"

Ricky clutched the phone, his brain flashing memories at him—Liam in his bed, Phil in his bed, Liam talking about strangling girls, Liam being sweet and funny and sexy, Liam— "What do you want?" His voice was hoarse.

"Are you still in touch with the others from Destiny's group at all? I thought maybe you might be since you still seem to be, I don't know, doing her bidding."

"I'm *not!*" This burst out of him. "I mean, I guess I am, but I can see it's her bidding, and I'm trying not to. It's only that it's hard."

"Okay," said Liam softly. "Okay, I didn't mean that as an accusation. Just… are you in touch or not?"

Tyler touched his knee. "Who is it?"

On impulse, Ricky pulled the phone away from his ear and put it on speaker. "Not really, no. Just Tyler, but he left, and he's not in touch with them either."

"Shit," said Liam. "Well… never mind, then, I guess."

"Is that Liam Emerson?" said Tyler.

"Someone's with you." Liam's voice had changed.

"Why are you asking me if I'm in touch with Destiny's group?" said Ricky.

"It's Haysle," said Liam, and there was a quaver in his voice.

"What about Haysle?" Ricky had always liked Haysle. He didn't want anything bad to happen to her.

"Is it Tyler with you, you said?" said Liam. "Tyler, are you in touch with the group?"

"The group doesn't care about Haysle Dawson," said Tyler.

"No, I know," said Liam. "She was captured by Finn, and he took her to the cabin in Virginia, the one where he used to… I don't know if you ever went there, but Destiny owned it. And now they're gone, and they seem to have driven off in a van that's registered to Mick."

"Mick?" said Tyler. "He might have wanted… revenge against Phineas."

"Right," piped up Ricky. "You were telling me that they thought he stole Destiny's energy. Maybe they were going to try to get it back."

"Wait, are you saying that the cult—uh, the group—could have taken Finn and Haysle? Because I thought maybe that Finn went back and took a van from the group—"

"If he went back there, they wouldn't have let him leave," said Tyler. "We were all armed, you know? We never used the guns on other people. They were there for us to sacrifice ourselves, but it's not like we weren't all well-versed in firearms."

"Shit," said Liam again. "Where would they go?"

"Maybe Delaware?" said Tyler. "Destiny thought certain places had power, and she thought that house outside of Branwen College had been soaking in energy from the very beginning, and if they were trying to release Phineas's energy, sacrifice him, they might go there."

"Thank you," said Liam. "And Ricky... I didn't... I wasn't helping Finn kill people. I wouldn't have asked you to—"

"Don't," said Ricky, defensive, annoyed. "Let's not do that."

"Right." Liam hesitated. "Right," he said again, and then he hung up.

HAYSLE RAN BEHIND Finn, and the two ran and ran, further into the woods. This area was sparsely populated but there were other houses out here.

One came into view, and she tried to swerve towards it, but Finn stopped her, saying that he was not going back to jail, and he yanked her off with him to keep going further into the woods.

Haysle tried to convince herself that the person in this house would have heard the gunfire, been alarmed, and called the police, but she couldn't make herself believe it. It was nothing for people out in the country to hear gunfire. People shot guns in the woods all the time, for hunting or for target practice or for sport.

No one was coming for her.

Eventually, they were both out of breath, and they stopped in a small clearing, the moon shining down overhead over both of them, and she gazed up into its silvery light and panted, keeping Finn in the periphery of her vision, wary.

He leaned up against a tree trunk, hugging the rifle to his chest. "So, you expect me to believe you're just going to have my baby, Haysle?"

She leveled her gaze at him, still trying to steady her breath. "Yes."

"Bullshit."

"Why wouldn't I?" she said.

"It's Liam's," he said. "I know it's Liam's—"

"No," she said. "It is not."

"Well, between the two of you… No way is he going to let you have another man's—"

"Yours?" she said. "Let's not be stupid here, Finn. He's not going to mind."

Finn pushed off the tree trunk and started for her. "Liam can be a little slutty, but he doesn't like sharing, not really. No one does."

"With you? He likes it." She swallowed. "I want to assure you, Finn, no matter what happens, we'll take care of your child. I swear that to you. That's the one thing I'll give you."

"You're giving me things?" He was coming closer.

"Just that," she said. "I already told you that I intend to be there when you die, and that I'm going to laugh and that will be the last thing you hear."

He closed the last bit of distance between them. "I think it's going to be the other way around. But, no. I won't laugh when you're dying. I would never do that."

"Right, I've watched you kill women, and you're *so* respectful about it."

"I try to make it quick and painless," he said. "I don't get off on pain, Haysle, that's at least one thing about me."

She laughed, a long, loud ridiculous laugh that echoed against the moon. "Right, Finn, you're a sweetheart." And that was when she moved.

Her leg went out and she kicked the gun out of his grasp and at the same time, she stabbed him with the pocket knife.

He grunted.

She pulled the small knife out and stuck it back in again. She stabbed and stabbed, jerky movements, poking him wherever she could get the blade in, just one after the other.

Until he got her hand and squeezed her wrist and made

her drop it.

She clawed at his face.

He grunted.

She drove her elbow, twisting herself almost painfully, into the wounds she'd made.

He cried out.

It was enough, and she wrenched away from him, staggering over to pick up the rifle. She tried the bolt action, but it wouldn't move—she didn't understand it—it wasn't like a police gun—she'd never been hunting—and she just flipped the thing around and drove the butt of it into his face.

He stumbled backwards. His noise was bleeding.

She jammed it into his face again.

He shrieked.

She swung the rifle over her shoulder and began bludgeoning him with it, smacking it into his flesh, hitting bone, blood spattering everywhere.

He flailed out, reaching for her, but he didn't connect. He grunted, down on one knee.

She hit him again and again and again.

Eventually, he collapsed.

She nudged him with her foot.

His face and head were like raw meat. She'd hit him a lot.

She went over and found the pocket knife. She wiped the blade on his pants, folded it up, and put it in her pocket. Dragging the rifle along with her, she left him behind.

She made her way back through the woods, glancing behind herself every now and again. She might have killed him. He'd looked dead. He probably wasn't coming after her, but... well... there was no telling what might happen.

I didn't laugh, she thought. *Oops.*

She'd been concentrating really hard on hitting him.

Eventually, she made it back to the house.

She made her way to the back door and made a fist and pounded against it.

There were no lights on in the house. It was silent and still.

She pounded again.

Waited.

No answer.

Dragging the rifle through the dead leaves that covered the ground around this house in the woods, she walked around and peered inside a window.

Inside, all the furniture was covered in sheets.

"Fuck," she said.

It was probably a summer house, a place where people came to be out in the woods and get away from it all. No one was there right now, in the late, cold fall.

She kept walking.

She walked and walked and walked.

At some point, she could see the road, the one that led back to town. How long would it take her to walk all the way back to town?

Maybe a long time, she thought, and she should stay in the woods, because the members of the cult might be going up and down the road, looking for her.

She walked a long while after that.

And when a car came down the road, her first instinct was to hide, thinking it was Mick and the others coming back.

But something about headlights and the shape of it let her know it wasn't that mini-van, and she hadn't seen any other cars and—

It was probably a stupid move, but she hurled herself forward, waving down the car, and it jerked to a stop and two people got out, and it was Mitch Clark and Liam.

Liam ran for her, pulling her into his arms, kissing her eyebrow, breathing her name into her skin.

She clung to him.

Liam pulled back. "Where's Finn? Where's Mick?"

She showed him the rifle. "We got away from Mick. We went in the woods. I think I killed Finn. I hit and hit him and he didn't get up."

"Where?" said Liam.

"Where?" she said.

"In the woods?" said Liam. "Can you point the direction?"

"I..." She furrowed her brow and pointed. "But we should get backup. Why didn't you call for the local police?"

Liam shoved her at Clark. "Take care of her."

"Liam?" She watched as Liam darted off into the woods. "Liam, what are you doing?"

"Get back here, Emerson," said Clark.

Liam ignored them both and disappeared into the trees.

Clark groaned. "I really don't like that guy."

"WE CALLED THE local police, but they were already checking out the bunker in town, and they didn't have anyone else on duty to go out here. They said they'd send someone as soon as they could," Clark was saying.

"So, it's just us," she said.

"It's just me," he said, looking her over. "You, um, have obviously been through hell."

"Well, I'm used to it," she said. "There are five of them, one man and four women. They're all armed. We need backup if we're going to go in there. It would be stupid to go in on our own."

"Uh, you're not going in anywhere," said Clark. "Can you back up and tell me about Slater? What do you mean you hit him?"

"With the gun." She held it up. "Would you believe I can't figure out how to get the damned thing cocked?"

Clark took it from her and struggled with it for a second. He set it down. "It think it's jammed."

"Oh," she said, nodding.

"We should go after Emerson," said Clark. "My priority is Slater."

"Not the crazed, violent cult members with guns?"

He sighed. "All right, fine. I'll get on the horn, and I'll rouse someone to send us a few more officers so that we can—"

A volley of gunshots all at once.

They exchanged a glance and then both darted back into the car.

Clark pulled the door closed and put on his seat belt, and Haysle followed suit. They sped off down the road.

"There, it's there," said Haysle. "That's the turn."

Clark careened into it, kicking up dust and dead leaves and then they were bumping and bouncing down the unpaved driveway, which was riddled with potholes.

Ahead of them, they could see the flames of the bonfire.

Then, they saw the first body.

Clark skidded the car to a stop.

They both got out and ran for the fire.

They'd all shot themselves.

Of course they had.

All five of them, splayed out and motionless as the the flames reflected on their skin.

Haysle put her hand over her mouth.

CHAPTER TWENTY-EIGHT

FINN WOKE TO pain and the trickle of cool water against his wounded skin.

He groaned, lifting his head, trying to make sense of what was happening.

"Shh." It was Liam's voice. "Don't try to move."

Finn lifted his head anyway. He was in a bathtub. There were lit candles on the sink across the room. The faucet was on, but the water coming out of it was cold.

"Sorry," said Liam. "The hot water heater hasn't warmed things up yet. This house had the water turned off and the electricity, and I had to run around doing all of that. I wanted to take you to the bunker, but I couldn't figure out how to get you there. This'll have to do. It's not as poetic, but..." He dabbed a wet washcloth against Finn's face.

Finn winced.

"Yeah, she got you good," said Liam. "Don't worry. I'll get you cleaned up. Just relax."

Finn eyed him. "What's going on?"

Liam continued to dab at his face. "I'm really glad you didn't hurt Haysle, Finn."

Finn snorted, laying his head back. "I thought I had to."

"No," said Liam. "I'm going to do it. Just like you wanted."

"I thought I had to push you—"

"It's happening."

Finn's heart suddenly started to race.

"Relax," said Liam again, his voice soothing.

"I can't." Finn shut his eyes, though, and lay back against the lip of the tub. He let Liam continue to clean him. That went on for a while, silent and slow, the water, the washcloth, the blood swirling down the drain. Finally, Finn said, "She tried to tell me it was my baby."

"It is," said Liam.

Finn opened his eyes. "You don't have to lie to me right now."

"I'm not lying," said Liam. "It's yours. So, see, it's going to be okay. You have a legacy now. You don't have to go back to jail, and you and I did Destiny together, and you got to kill with me. You got everything you wanted." He rinsed blood out of the washcloth, and wet it again, and then began to drag it over Finn's chest.

Finn's breath hitched. "I… I just… I don't know if I'm ready."

"No, I know," said Liam, washcloth going lower, over Finn's stomach. "I know. It doesn't have to be right away. We can work up to it. I'm nervous too." Liam brushed the washcloth this way and that. "Tell me about the video of me killing Destiny. You got that backed up on the cloud somewhere?"

Finn let out a laugh. "You're worried about that, tiger? You know you couldn't believe anything I said anyway. But you can be sure that I don't have anyone else I'm in contact with or anything like that. It's not going live if, uh, if something happens to…"

The washcloth was lower still, and Liam wrapped it around Finn's cock.

Finn felt a tremor of pleasure go through him. He shut his eyes. "Are you going to fuck me first?"

"Do you want me to?"

"You wouldn't do it after, would you?"

A chuckle from Liam. "Uh, no."

"Okay, then. I want you to."

"You want me inside you?"

Finn nodded.

"Okay," said Liam.

The washcloth stroked Finn, and the texture of the fabric was rough and sweet and he kept his eyes closed and let Liam tease him stiff. He moaned softly, letting his hips buck a little against the ministrations, until they abruptly stopped.

Finn opened his eyes.

Liam offered him his hand. "Not in the bathtub."

Finn put his hand into the other man's and let him help him up.

Arms around each other, they left the bathroom and Liam brought him into a bedroom, where there were more candles set up on a sheet-swathed dresser.

"You set up the candles. You planned it," said Finn softly. "You planned to fuck me."

"I planned it for here," said Liam. "I didn't think the bathtub… there's a certain practicality to doing it there, I guess, but I thought it'd be nicer someplace soft."

Finn looked back at him. "How long have you been planning it?"

Liam shook his head. "I don't know. Since we were kids, maybe."

Finn's breath hitched. "I don't know if I want you to."

"I know," said Liam. "I know that."

Finn ran a hand through his hair. He winced, because his face was so badly hurt. "I mean, I *want* it, I do, I just… I'm scared."

"I think that's probably normal," said Liam.

Finn turned to look at him. "Really? Since we were kids?"

"I don't know if I was seriously planning it then," said Liam. "Maybe, I was, though. After what happened with Destiny… after what I thought I did… after what you did to me…" He shifted on his feet. "This is happening, Finn. It can be like this, with the candles and the bed, or it can be uglier. But it's happening."

Finn swallowed. He realized that he was naked and Liam was dressed. He looked down at his erection, which seemed to only have gotten more erect during this conversation, and that made him smile a little, because of the perversity of it, which made things better for him, always had. He looked up at Liam, and his heart beat faster—in apprehension, in excitement, in whatever it was of dread he could even of feel, which wasn't as much as other people. The dread and excitement entwined, bursting through him, going straight to the root of his groin. "How do you want me?"

Liam licked his lips. He rolled his head on his shoulders. "Lay down on the bed."

"On my stomach?"

Liam's jaw twitched. "On your back." His voice was ragged. He tugged his shirt over his head.

Finn lay down. He drew in a breath and looked at the ceiling and then down over his naked body, at his hard cock, pointing straight at the ceiling, and at Liam, who was unbuttoning his pants.

Liam was older now, but Finn remembered his younger body, remembered the way it had been the first time he'd put his lips against Liam's, how forbidden and strange and good it had been to kiss him.

Liam kicked his pants away. He was hard too. That was gratifying.

Finn watched as Liam picked up a tube of lube from the dresser. "You brought that with you?"

"It was actually in the house. I thought I'd use oil or something otherwise," said Liam, settling on the bed, between Finn's legs. "I'm not using a condom, not for this, so it's not like it matters."

Finn tensed, and now his breath started to go wildly out of rhythm, and he had a thought about fighting back, about turning this into something else, and he thought if it came down to pitting his strength against Liam's, he would win.

The lube was cold and thick, but Liam's finger was warm.

Finn shuddered. He looked away, up at the ceiling again.

Liam's hand on his cock again, a gentle squeeze. "Relax."

Finn let out a noisy breath. He shut his eyes. "How are you going to do it?"

"That's a surprise," said Liam.

Finn shuddered again, a jerk that brought him off the bed. He clenched around Liam's finger, which was halfway into him at this point.

"I'd tell you," said Liam's voice, "but I think you'll fight it if you know. I can't have you doing that."

"You won't… you wouldn't do it messy, I don't think. You wouldn't like that."

"Mmm." Liam urged another finger inside him.

Finn groaned. "But you wouldn't… I don't think you're going to try it with brute strength either. I'm not Destiny, and I'm not—"

"Shh." Two fingers, squirming in deeper and deeper. "Open up, Finn. Let me in."

Finn shuddered again.

"You want me to get you real loose, or you want to be nice and tight for me?"

"Whatever you…" Finn opened his eyes and looked at him. "Whatever's good for you."

Liam's eyes were half-lidded.

Finn was starting to shake. His whole body was shaking. "Liam…" It was a whimper.

Liam removed both of his fingers and climbed over him, caging him in. He kissed him.

Finn moaned into his mouth.

Liam kissed Finn's chin and his chest and his belly and then the tip of his cock. "You want to beg for it?"

Finn's mouth was dry. "I…"

"Call me tiger," said Liam, stroking Finn's cock. "Ask nicely."

"Please, tiger," said Finn. "Please…" He didn't finish.

And then Liam was there, pressing inside of him, his hand wrapped around Finn's cock, still stroking him as he claimed him.

They were face to face, joined, and Liam panted over him. "Good boy, Finn," he breathed.

Finn shuddered again and then he gave himself over to the pleasure.

They moved together, and Finn writhed against the bed,

and he flung out his arms and that was when he found the knife under the pillow. He pulled it out.

Liam let go of Finn's cock to seize his wrist, pinning his hand down against the bed. He gritted his teeth.

Finn was still holding the knife, but he couldn't move his hand. He picked up his other hand and put it on Liam's face. He dragged his fingers down over Liam's features, and all the while Liam was fucking him, Liam was thrusting into him, Liam was deep inside him, and then he dug his fingers into Liam's neck.

Liam pried Finn's fingers away from the knife, his face a mask of determination or pleasure or something else... Finn thought maybe he'd seen that expression on Liam's face only once before, when they were killing Destiny, and it made something inside him go hot as the dread and excitement within him twined *very* tight.

"Now, now, Finn," Liam said in a ravaged voice, "you wanted me to do it."

"I changed my mind," said Finn, digging his fingers tighter into Liam's flesh.

"Too late," rasped Liam, and the knife was a glinting flash of silver and Finn tried to buck Liam off and then the knife was coming for him, the tip rushing down and there was a bright spurt of pain and then—

EPILOGUE

HAYSLE YANKED OPEN the door, and she slapped Liam across the face.

He put his hand to his jaw, eyeing her. "Good to see you too."

"It's been three *days*," she said. "Where have you been?"

He shook his head. "You don't want to know that." He eased his way past her, into the house.

After finding the bodies all around the bonfire, she'd been with Clark at the scene until dawn. Everything was photographed and all the evidence was bagged and tagged and all the bodies were carted off by the coroner, and Liam was nowhere to be found.

She and Clark went into the woods, and she found the clearing where she'd left Finn, and there was blood on the ground, and it looked like someone had dragged a body out of there.

They tried to follow the trail, but they lost it, and they went wandering around in the woods for the better part of the morning, but they didn't find any sign of either Liam or Finn.

She was exhausted, so she had gotten a room in a local hotel and slept.

And then there were statements to give, and she'd gone through her story more than once, and then gone back to the damned woods, looking for Liam.

Where the fuck was Liam?

At some point, she knew.

Liam was dead.

Liam had gone out and found Finn, and Finn had killed him.

That was when she went home.

And then, now, here he was, the door just opening, and him just walking inside.

She went after him, grabbing him, wrapping her arms around him from behind, her voice coming out as a sob. "I thought he killed you."

"No," said Liam. "He was never going to kill me."

She let go of him. Something in his voice…

He turned around, letting out a noisy breath. He touched her face, tracing the outline of her cheek and jaw, affectionate.

"I *do* want to know," she said.

He shook his head. "No, you don't. All you need to know is that he's gone."

She pulled away. "Liam. What did you do?"

"Don't," he said.

She hugged herself.

He pressed close. He smelled a little bit like bleach, and she shuddered, knowing that meant he'd been cleaning up… cleaning up a… He kissed her forehead. "It's going to get better now. It's over." Then he let go of her.

Her legs didn't feel strong enough to hold her. Her hand jerked out and she pressed her palm into the wall, and she stayed there, watching as he walked deeper into the house, shrugging out of the jacket he was wearing.

"Now, you can go back to work," he said. "You said you didn't want to do homicide anymore, so maybe you can transfer to robbery again, and—"

"I've been thinking about that."

"Yeah?" He rounded a bend, going into the living room, and he was only a disembodied voice.

"Yeah." Her voice was trembling. "I, um, I can't go back to work at the Cape Christopher Department, not after everything they know about me. It would feel like they could see through my clothes."

"If that's how you feel," came his voice.

"I want to try being a private detective." She raised her voice. "I want to look for missing people. I like finding things."

"Sounds good," he called back.

She squared her shoulders. She stood up straight, and she walked down the hall, feeling a little odd, as if her head was attached to her body with a string and that everything was shaking a little too much.

She lurched into the living room, where Liam was sitting on the couch, bent over, both of his hands thrust into his hair.

She kept moving towards him. "I'm keeping the baby."

"I know."

"You'll…" She sat down next to him. "That's why you did it, isn't it? For me. For our baby?"

He lifted his face and looked at her. He nodded.

She picked up his hand and draped his arm around her. She snuggled into him. "You're going to be a really great dad."